Innocent Hearts

Innocent Hearts

Radclyffe

Yellow Rose Books
a Division of
RENAISSANCE ALLIANCE PUBLISHING, INC.
Nederland, Texas

ISBN 1-930928-32-7

First Printing 2002

9 8 7 6 5 4 3 2 1

Cover design by Mary D. Brooks

Published by:

Renaissance Alliance Publishing, Inc.
PMB 238, 8691 9th Avenue
Port Arthur, TX 77642

Find us on the World Wide Web at
http://www.rapbooks.biz

Printed in the United States of America

Acknowledgments:

There are always more people to thank than I can name, and many of the readers who have supported me throughout the creation of this work are known to me only through the Internet. To those individuals around the world who have written to me about this and other stories, I can only say that yours are the voices that inspire. Never underestimate the importance of your feedback.

Tomboy, JB, and Athos did the lion's share of the beta reading on this one, and as always, you were each superb. Not only do you polish the prose, you provide me with personal support, for which I will always be grateful. Thank you, HS (B,PT), for the care and nurturing of the Radlist, and Laney, for the dedicated and sensitive editing.

Lee deserves my deepest gratitude for her willingness to share our life with the many characters who occupy my mind and for never failing to encourage me when I falter.

For Lee
For All the Dreams

Prologue

Martha Beecher looked up in surprise as her husband rushed into the drawing room waving a piece of paper in his hand, shouting, "Martha!"

"My goodness, Martin. What is it?" She put her needlepoint aside and stared at him in alarm.

"It's from Thaddeus," he exclaimed, his joyful expression making him look much younger than his forty-odd years. "He's talked to the wagon master of the next group leaving for the Northern Territory. We can join them, he says. He'll arrange everything as soon as we send word."

She smiled shakily, trying to quell the quick surge of anxiety as she thought of leaving her home for an unknown destination, surrounded by strangers for months while traveling over hundreds of miles of wild unpopulated land. How impossible it had all seemed less than a year ago when a letter had arrived from Martin's boyhood friend, Thaddeus Schroeder, extolling the virtues of the unsettled west and the Montana Territory in particular.

Pure air, clear skies, and no crowds or stench of factories, Thaddeus had written. *The war that has divided the nation is a distant thunder here in the northern territories. Out here, any*

man can claim land just for the tending of it and make his for-
tune with the sweat of his brow. The newspaper is growing every
day, Martin, just like our fine town, and I need a partner to help
me run it. I want you to be that man.

At first the idea of moving west had seemed nothing more
than a wild dream. True, she had known for some time that Martin was growing steadily more discontented with his teaching
position and equally dissatisfied with the changes in their life
that the war and industrialization had brought. More and more
people had flooded the Northern cities from the impoverished
countryside and the decimated South. They were looking for
work in the factories that had sprung up everywhere, crowding
the landscape and fouling the air. The swelling population had
resulted in an increase in crime and disease, too.

The offer of a partnership on a newspaper and a chance at a
new life had truly energized her husband. But what did they
know of frontier living—they who had never been further west
than Albany? When she had accompanied him to the public
library to study a map of the new territory, searching for the
town that had then been only a name, she realized that Martin
had already set his heart on leaving.

"But Martin, it doesn't even look settled," she began cautiously, trying to smother her look of horror. All she could appreciate was a vast open area marked by very little evidence of
civilization.

"The towns are small and far apart, my dear," he said.
"They started out as mining camps during the rush west to find
gold. But they are growing larger every day."

"It's so far..."

"Only the last half of the trip would be difficult." He traced
the route of the Oregon Trail with his finger, oblivious to his
wife's reservations. "Thaddeus says about four months altogether, and the roads are good all the way into Nebraska. Of
course, we would have to leave most of the furniture behind...But
Martha. Think of it. It's a brand new country out there, just
beginning to grow. With the Homestead Act promising land to
any man who lives on it, a whole new world is going to spring up*

*overnight. We could be a part of something grand, and the news-
paper would be at the heart of it.*"

Martha Beecher had tried then to share his enthusiasm, and
she had gradually accepted that they would someday go. Now,
looking at the flush of excitement on her husband's face, she
knew that the time was at hand.

"We must settle on what to do about Kate, Martin," she said
quietly, struggling to hide her apprehension. "If we are to leave
soon, we must decide. She is eighteen now and at the age when a
girl should be marrying. How can we ask her to leave behind all
that Boston has to offer for a life in a place we know nothing
of?"

She knew how hard it would be for her husband to part with
Kate, especially when it might be years before they saw their
daughter again, and she saw his hesitation. "I'll go anywhere
that makes you happy, Martin," she added, keeping her deepest
fears to herself. "If you are happy, I will be, too."

*But our Kate? Don't we owe her more? Who knows what
type of men we might find in such an unsettled place. Kate is
much too refined to become the wife of a shopkeeper, or worse,
a...farmer.*

Sitting beside his wife on the settee, Martin took her hand.
"Martha, I don't know how I know, but I feel certain that this
move will be right for us." His voice was thick with emotion and
his eyes grew cloudy with concern. "But perhaps you are right
about Kate. A young woman like her, giving up all of this—the
dances, the parties, the finer things. Perhaps it would be too
much of a hardship."

Doubt had crept into his voice, and Martha could not bear
that. She took his large hand into her small one and said with
sudden determination, "Kate can stay here with my sister Ellen
until she marries. She is almost of the age when she would be
leaving us soon for a husband anyway. Perhaps it will be sooner,
that's all."

Her calm, strong words comforted him, and he smiled again.
"I suppose, after all, we should ask her."

⌘ ❖ ♦ ❖ ♦ ❖ ♦ ⌘

Kate Beecher looked up from her book as her parents walked into the room. She was seated in front of the fire, the flickering glow illuminating her bold features and shimmering waves of shoulder length hair. She smiled at them fondly, a question in her dark eyes. "You look like you have news," she said in her rich, full voice.

"Kate, darling," Martha began tentatively, "your father and I have talked at great length about this move west, and we feel that we should go." She glanced at Martin, who was strangely silent, and took his hand. "We are not sure what lies ahead, but it will be very different from our life here. We are prepared to leave, but you're a young woman now, and this is the only life you have known. There are many opportunities here and comforts that you might never have in Montana. The theater, opera, your friends..." Her voice trailed off, and she looked intently at her daughter, who seemed to be struggling not to interrupt.

"You two!" Kate exclaimed, her eyes alive with laughter. "Do you really think I would let you go without me and miss this great adventure? There is nothing I care for enough to keep me here, and no one I care for more than you. I want to come. I have always felt that this is *not* where I belong. Perhaps I will find that I belong in Montana."

Her father looked at her with his mouth agape. Surely there was no young lady either more popular or more accomplished than his daughter. She had many friends and not a few would-be suitors. In addition to her dark-eyed, black-haired beauty, her wit and intelligence quickly won her acceptance in any circle. *Not belong here? Preposterous.*

Martha ignored the excitement, so like Martin's, in her daughter's voice. Kate had altogether too much of her father's adventurous spirit. Alas, Martha blamed herself for allowing Kate, as a child, to spend so much time with Martin, accompanying him everywhere, and not emphasizing enough that Kate needed to prepare for a life as a wife and mother.

She had warned Martin that the college library was no place for a girl to be spending so much time. Although she accepted a young lady's need to read and write, she was concerned that Kate spent far too many hours alone with her books. Martha finally had to put her foot down after Martin had given in to Kate's demands that he teach her about his photographic pastime. A dark room filled with foul smelling chemicals was no place for a girl, even if Kate was a natural at image making, as Martin so proudly proclaimed. If Kate needed something to occupy her time, she could learn needlepoint.

"There are not likely to be the prospects for your future on the uncivilized frontier that you would find here," Martha insisted. She looked to her husband for support, but found none. She continued bluntly, "There are so many promising young men here. You must think of that, Kate."

Kate spoke carefully, because she knew that her mother could insist that she remain behind. "Whether I am here or there, Mother, I will only make a match that feels right in my heart. I do not believe that love is dictated by geography. You know there is no one here for whom I have any attachment."

That was precisely what concerned Martha most. There had been more than one suitable gentleman to appear at their door. Kate had received each one politely and had just as politely sent each one on his way. But before Martha could protest further, Martin interceded; in truth, he could not bear the thought of leaving for a new life without his daughter.

"Are you sure, Kate?" he asked. "This journey will be long and difficult."

"Quite sure, Father," she answered, feeling the first thrill of new possibility. "Make no mistake; I want to go."

Chapter
1

New Hope, Montana Territory
May 1865

Martin Beecher halted the wagon on a knoll overlooking a sprawling town that lay nestled in a valley hewn from the eastern reaches of the Rockies. He sat forward eagerly, anxious for his first glimpse of their new home.

"There it is, Martha. We've finally arrived," he exclaimed as he reached for his wife's hand. "Kate, come look!"

Martha sat beside him on the rough wagon bench, stiff from the lingering chill of the spring night barely past, bundled to the nose in a heavy blanket. She couldn't help but think that in Boston the tulips would be in bloom, whereas in the valley below, snow still lingered.

Kate pushed between them from the rear of the covered wagon, one gloved hand on each of their shoulders. Despite the cold, she was bareheaded and her glossy hair shone darkly in the bright sunlight. She surveyed the scene before her eagerly, oblivious to her mother's expression of dread. There were perhaps a dozen buildings in all on either side of a rutted dirt road that was clearly Main Street. She shielded her eyes in the early morning sun to make out other houses scattered along the outskirts of the

town and further into the foothills, wherever homesteaders had
settled.

"Is that the town?" she asked, her voice alight with an echo
of her father's enthusiasm. "Are we here?"

She could hardly believe that they had finally arrived. Once
the decision had been made to leave Boston, everything had happened so quickly. Her father had resigned from the college and
sold their house at a good profit. Her mother had donated most
of their garments to several charities that provided for those who
were displaced or left behind by the rapid pace of progress. Silk
dresses and finery would be useless in a small frontier town, so
Martha had purchased simple, sensible traveling clothes for the
family. Taking Thaddeus' advice, they had decided to leave
almost all the furniture behind as well.

Kate and her parents set out from their home before the last
graying snows of winter had melted from the streets, planning to
follow the warm winds west. Like so many hopeful travelers of
the time, they had no idea what truly lay ahead.

The first segment of their journey had been relatively comfortable as they traveled by rail to Independence, Missouri.
There the regular railroad service ended, and that was the point
where most expeditions proceeding to the western territories
began. In the previous year, 1864, a Congress still divided by the
uneasy sentiments of war had passed the second Pacific Railroad
Act, allocating funds for the construction of a transcontinental
railroad. Shortly after the surrender of the Confederacy, the
Union Pacific railroad began moving westward, rail by rail, but
it hadn't yet been completed when Kate and her family set out.

In Missouri, they had joined the wagon train, both for safety
and to afford company for Martha and Kate. They had many rea-
sons in the coming weeks to be grateful for Thaddeus' experience and the arrangements he had made for them in advance,
especially since none of them, not even Martin, had ever been
beyond the confines of civilized eastern society. Their trek
across the mid-west had been in a ten by five foot covered wagon
that had barely accommodated the three of them, six stout trunks
containing all their remaining worldly goods, several boxes of
books, and a wardrobe of her mother's with which Martha had

refused to part.

As they slowly labored over narrow rutted trails that often threatened to capsize their Prairie Schooner, spring had first overtaken, then threatened to pass them by somewhere along the northern trail through the Great Plains heading to the newly created Montana Territory. Even as they had traversed the flat lands and climbed toward the eastern slopes of the Rockies, the last snows had retreated. Riverbeds and streams swelled to overflowing, making the last few weeks of their trek arduous for animals and humans alike.

The journey had been longer than expected and harsher than they had imagined. The Overland Trail had been littered with the possessions of families that had not been as well prepared for the journey as they. Sadly, there were more than a few hastily erected markers remembering fellow travelers who, due to accident or disease, would never reach the land of promise they had envisioned so hopefully.

Despite the dark moments, Martin's unfailing optimism and Kate's buoyant sense of anticipation had kept all their spirits from flagging. Now, with Boston receding into a distant memory, Kate looked down upon the tiny town and felt that her life was truly about to begin.

"Are we really here?" Kate asked again.

"Yes indeed, darling Kate," Martin answered cheerfully. "At last—New Hope, Montana."

"I am so glad. I can't wait to meet the Schroeders. Do you know which is their house?"

He laughed, delighted by her eagerness. Perhaps he needn't have worried about her after all. He pointed toward the spire-peaked, square clapboard building nearest them. "That's the church. Thaddeus said it was the first building they raised, and next to that the schoolhouse, I imagine. The Schroeders live somewhere near the center of town. I'm sure that we will have no trouble finding them."

Kate did not see the stark simplicity of the town and the wild countryside as something to fear, as her mother did. Like her father, she saw a chance that her life might be more than she had been raised to believe it would be.

She thought about the last year of her life in Boston, the year that most girls her age remembered as the most exciting. It had not been for her. She had attended the required coming out parties, the afternoon socials, and the debutante balls. She had been properly introduced and had made the proper connections. It had been pleasant, but somehow it struck her as frivolous, too. She found the conversations considered appropriate between young ladies and gentlemen dull and the attentions of would-be suitors tiresome. Perhaps here she would find that there was more substance and fulfillment to life than that.

She gripped her father's shoulder harder. "And the newspaper office, where you'll be working? That's here, too?"

"One of the very first in the territory," Martin pronounced proudly, throwing his arms around his wife. "Just think of it."

His excitement was so boundless, and so simple, that Martha's heart lifted at the sight of his pleasure. She returned his hug and said softly with more conviction than she felt, "It will be wonderful, darling. I'm sure of it."

"Yes," Kate whispered fervently. "It will be."

Chapter
2

Martha was astounded at their reception. Thaddeus Schroeder's wife, Hannah, took them into their home as if they had been long-awaited relatives.

"John! John Emory! You carry those bags upstairs while I get these folks something to eat!" Hannah bellowed merrily, while herding the Beecher family into her living room. She was a head shorter than Martha and almost twice her size, with a round face and twinkling blue eyes. She had none of the pampered look of the Boston matrons Martha had called friends, and her nearly palpable energy threatened to overwhelm the sedate Easterner.

"Oh no, really," Martha protested, looking to her husband and daughter for support. "We only stopped to let you know we had arrived. I'm sure Martin can find us suitable lodging at the...uh...hotel."

"Don't you believe it," Hannah responded earnestly, moving books and papers from the worn couch in the sitting area. "That hotel is sure to be full with cowboys in for the week's end or worse, and it's no place for you folks to be staying. You'll stay right here with us 'til you get settled. We've plenty of room and a couple more mouths to feed is no hardship."

Kate recognized the look of consternation on her mother's face and took her arm, whispering softly, "Mother, I think we should accept Mrs. Schroeder's hospitality. It's been so long since we've slept anywhere but the wagon. Besides, it will give Father a chance to talk things over with Mr. Schroeder, too."

"That's right, my dear," Martin added. "I'm sure that Thaddeus has suggestions for a place we might acquire."

Hannah nodded. "That he has. Now, I'll get busy heating water because I should think you'll be wanting proper baths along about now."

"Why don't you rest awhile, and I'll help Mrs. Schroeder in the kitchen," Kate urged, a slightly worried expression on her face.

The journey had taken its toll on all of them, but none so much as her mother. She had lost weight and seemed more fragile than Kate could ever recall. It did not occur to Kate that *she* had been the one to change. In the months since they had last seen Boston, she had endured physical hardship and witnessed death in all its cruelty without faltering. She had helped her father when helping was needed, and she was stronger for it.

"Perhaps Mrs. Schroeder and I can make some of that tea we've been saving," Kate suggested.

"Right you are, child. You come with me," Hannah said with authority and bustled out.

Kate followed, as eager for the chance to talk with Hannah Schroeder about the town as she was for the promise of a bath.

Martha turned to her husband in dismay. "Martin?"

He looked back good-naturedly and turned his hands up. "I guess it's decided."

⌘ ❖ ◆ ❖ ◆ ❖ ◆ ⌘

A few days became more than a week before Kate's father decided upon a house on the southern edge of town. The dwelling was a modest but sound two-story wood structure, and Kate was especially pleased that there was a small room adjacent to hers that she might use for her photography. It was a brisk walk to work for Martin and near enough to the other townspeople for Martha and Kate to socialize. Kate knew that he was worried that she and her mother would be lonely. As it turned out, his concerns were unfounded.

While their new home was being readied, they remained at the Schroeder's, during which time Martha and Kate were besieged with visitors. Newcomers, especially Easterners, were a rarity, and everyone wanted to meet them. Kate enjoyed herself thoroughly, and she found herself accepting invitations to tea and something on Saturday afternoons called a quilting circle. Martha found the easy familiarity of the women both captivating and a little unnerving.

"My goodness, they're quite intense, aren't they?" she gasped after one particularly busy morning of entertaining in the Schroeder living room.

"Oh, I think they're wonderful," Kate exclaimed. "I feel so welcome." She reached for her shawl and bag. "Mother, I asked John to show me more of the town this afternoon. We've been here for days, and I scarcely know what the place looks like. Would you like to come?"

"Not today, darling. I've had quite enough new experiences for one morning, thank you." Martha sank wearily to the sofa, sighing with relief.

Laughing, Kate leaned over to kiss her lightly on the cheek and said briskly, "All right. I'll be home soon. I promised I'd help Mrs. Schroeder with dinner."

⌘ ❖ ♦ ❖ ♦ ❖ ♦ ⌘

John Emory Schroeder was seventeen years old—tall, strong and sturdy. He was more than pleased to be strolling down Main Street with Miss Kate Beecher. He had never seen anyone quite as fetching as she, especially in that dress that was far finer than anything he had seen the girls in town wearing. He didn't think for a minute that she might ever take notice of someone like him, but just accompanying her increased his stature in the eyes of all his friends.

"This here is the main street, Miss Kate. We've got a general store, right over there, next to the livery, and the bank across from that, of course. Down yonder is the schoolhouse, and—"

"Wait, John. Just show me as we go, please, or I'll never remember a thing," Kate pleaded with a laugh, pushing back her bonnet to let the sun, strike her face. Her mother would disapprove of the effects on her skin, but Kate didn't care. She couldn't stand to be hidden away. It was almost the first of June, and the air was still crisp and cool, so unlike the muggy early summer days she recalled in the city.

"Oh right, sure," he said, blushing to the roots of his sandy-brown hair.

By the time they had walked the five blocks to the end of the central thoroughfare, Kate knew where women bought their dry goods and sewing materials, where the children went to school, and where the men from the surrounding ranches came to have a drink and spend their wages on a Friday night. Turning back, she was struck with the efficiency and order of the small town. Every need was met, simply and without embellishment. But the street was clean and the board sidewalk sturdy, and all the faces she passed were kind and friendly.

"Let's rest awhile, shall we?" she said suddenly, brushing off a place to sit on the bench in front of the dry goods store. "It's so beautiful today; I don't want to go back inside just yet."

"Why, uh, okay," John said, now at a loss for words. He sat down beside her on the bench and stretched his long legs out in front of him. He swallowed audibly several times, but when it became apparent that Kate did not require him to converse, he relaxed.

Kate didn't notice his discomfort. She was too engrossed with absorbing every detail of her new home. Everything was so different, right down to the hard packed earth of the street before her. Gone were the cobblestone roads and fine horse-drawn carriages that she was used to seeing. These common sights had been replaced by plain, board-sided wagons and heavy draft horses, accustomed to pulling loads of supplies or stubborn stumps, as their owners required. The houses, though carefully tended and built to last, were a far cry from the stone townhouses where Kate and her friends had lived.

Despite the stark utility of the place, she sensed an air of vitality and vigor she had not noticed in the staid surroundings of her former home. There was a steady stream of ranchers and homesteaders in and out of town loading wagons, men calling to one another as they led horses in and out of the livery, and women passing by on the sidewalks, laden with parcels. She couldn't help but feel a thrill of excitement to find herself indeed a part of this strange new world.

She watched another of the young cowboys who had been passing by all morning cross the street to the blacksmith's opposite her. She was coming to recognize the same purposeful gait and easy carriage that all the men seemed to have. Following the tall, lanky form clad in rough denim toward the corral, she was struck by the unusual refinement of the deeply tanned features. As he swept off his hat to wipe a sleeve across his brow, she caught sight of the thick, blond hair held back with a dark tie.

"Oh! My goodness," she cried in a startled voice. "That's a woman!"

"Huh?" John asked, rousing from his reverie. He had been nearly asleep beside her in the warm sun. "Who?"

Kate pointed in astonishment, quite forgetting that it was rude. "Right over there."

"Oh, that's just Jessie," John dismissed. "Her mare threw a shoe this morning, and she's coming to get her, I reckon." He finished, as if that settled things.

Kate stared openly at the woman, who was leaning one booted foot on the lower board of the railing fronting the corral, deep in conversation with the blacksmith. What startled Kate even more than her attire was the side arm holstered neatly against her muscular thigh.

"But she's wearing a gun," Kate insisted, amazed. She should have been scandalized, she supposed, but she was simply too surprised to be anything but curious.

"Why, I guess she'd better, riding into town alone, what with the way things are out on the range," John said matter-of-factly. "Settlers are fighting mad about expeditions crossing over their lands on the way to the Oregon gold fields, and my father says the miners are violating the treaties with the Indians, too. People are starting to get riled, and the marshal can't be expected to be everywhere, you know," he proclaimed with authority, clearly still echoing the words of his father.

"Yes, but...well, I mean...who *is* she?"

John turned to her, confused. "I told you. Name's Jessie Forbes. She has a ranch a few miles out of town. Does right well, too, so everybody says. She doesn't seem to have any trouble selling her horses. I wish I could get one of hers," he finished wistfully.

Kate turned to him, eyes full of wonder. "You mean she *owns* it?"

"Well, I reckon so, since her father died a ways back, and she's the only one left. I suppose she owns it."

Kate stared at the woman whose features were shadowed at the moment by the wide-brimmed Stetson that she wore. Now that Kate looked carefully, she could see that the body was not that of a young man. Jessie Forbes was lean and muscular to be sure, but there was a subtle curve to the hip and slenderness in the arms that betrayed her sex. And under the worn denim of her shirt, sweat-dampened in the back, there was a suggestive swell of breasts. Never in her life had Kate seen a woman wear pants, even in the confines of her own home.

She continued to stare until she realized that the woman was heading straight toward them, leading a beautiful chestnut mare. She quickly averted her gaze despite the fact that she desperately wanted to see Jessie up close. *This woman will think I have no manners at all, staring at her like a schoolboy.*

Kate heard the jangle of spurs grow louder, until suddenly the sound stopped and a shadow fell across the wooden sidewalk right in front of them. She found herself looking down at the dusty toes of two very well-worn boots.

Jessie threw the reins over the railing and took the two stairs up to the porch in one long stride.

"Howdy, Jessie," John said amiably.

"Afternoon, John," she answered as she stepped into the dry goods store.

Kate was surprised at the deep but melodious timbre of her voice. She glanced then at the horse standing quietly before them, taking in the well-ridden but still beautiful saddle engraved with an elegantly tooled *JF*. Her eyes widened slightly as she noticed the rifle tucked into a case on the right side. She turned to John with another question but stopped when she heard the spurs behind them again.

"Say, John, you can tell your dad I've got that colt down from the high country if he wants to ride out and see him sometime," Jessie said as she came through the door on her way out of the store before she noticed that Kate was about to speak. "Oh, sorry, I didn't mean to be interrupting."

Kate looked up into the bluest eyes she had ever seen. Her glance traveled quickly from the sun-bleached hair beneath the brim of the cowboy hat and over the strong cheekbones to a generous mouth and square chin. She dropped her gaze when she saw Jessie color slightly and felt her own face flame. *What has gotten into me?*

"Oh, it's okay, Jessie. You're not interrupting," John assured, warming to his role as guide. "This here is Miss Kate Beecher, and she's just come from Boston. Her dad and mine are going to run the paper together now."

Jessie reached up with a slim, long-fingered hand, browned from the sun, and quickly removed her hat. She looked down from what seemed to Kate to be a great height and said softly, "I'm pleased to meet you, Miss Beecher. I'm Jessie Forbes. You picked the right time of year to arrive in Montana. Spring and summer are mighty fine seasons." She smiled then, and her eyes flashed a gentle welcome.

Kate smiled back and held out her hand. "I believe it is easily the most beautiful country that I have ever seen, Miss Forbes."

Jessie took her hand in a firm but careful grip and replied, "Please call me Jessie." She held Kate's hand for an instant and then stepped back self-consciously. "Well, John, you give your dad that message. I'd best be getting along."

"Sure, Jessie. See you at the sale."

Though still slightly bedazzled, Kate followed the trim line of Jessie's back as she went quickly down the stairs and grasped the reins of her horse. Effortlessly, the rancher swung one long leg over the saddle and looked down at Kate almost shyly from her mount.

"Good luck to you, Miss Beecher."

"Thank you, Jessie," she replied, adding quickly, "My name is Kate."

Jessie smiled easily and tipped her hat once again.

"Good afternoon then, Miss Kate. John." And with that she swung her horse away and spurred her into an easy canter out of town.

John didn't notice Kate's quiet concentration as they walked slowly back to the house. As he continued to point out the local sights, Kate nodded absently, all the while reflecting on blue eyes and a fleeting smile, warmer than any she could ever recall.

Oh my, but what would they think of her *back in Boston,* Kate thought, unable to forget the odd encounter. She had imagined all manner of new discoveries on the frontier, but she had never dreamed of anything as intriguing as Jessie Forbes.

Chapter
3

Jessie turned slowly onto her back and gingerly shook each arm and then each leg. *I think I'm all intact, no thanks to anything but good fortune.* Her hat lay several feet away, where it had fallen when she landed on her face.

"Well, you won that round," she muttered good-naturedly as she looked up at the horse standing quietly over her. She got stiffly to her feet, dusted the dirt from her slightly tender backside, and stroked his long, sensitive nose. "How can any horse as friendly as you are be so hard to ride?"

She had acquired the roan stallion in trade several weeks before, and after letting him settle in for a few days, she had saddled him up for the first time. He had accepted the saddle and bridle amiably enough, but Jessie was no sooner seated than Rory had neatly deposited her on the ground. After the shock had passed, she had laughed heartily, thinking that the rancher who had left with two of her mares might have gotten the better part of the bargain. She would have to remember to invite him to the next big card game so she could even the score.

As the days passed, it had become apparent that Rory would indeed be a challenge. He had greeted her each time she approached with a friendly shake of his head and nuzzled her shoulder, looking for sugar or apples, but he would not let her ride him.

That afternoon she had walked him, fully saddled, for almost an hour. He had been well-mannered and obedient. As casually as possible, she had pulled him up and mounted him effortlessly. To her great amazement, he had responded instantly to her touch and walked easily about the corral. She had leaned forward to pat his neck and compliment him, which was when he had kicked his hind legs and catapulted her over his head.

"That was a nice fall you took there, Jess."

She turned to see her foreman leaning against the fence, watching her with just the hint of a smile. Jed Harper was raw-boned and weather-beaten, with the ageless face of someone who had lived all his life in the open.

"I'm glad it was you saw that and not one of the other men," she said with a rueful grin. "He's a smart one, this Rory."

Had it been anyone other than Jed who had witnessed her most recent defeat, Jessie would have been embarrassed. Jed, however, had been around as long as she could remember, and she had nothing to hide from him. She was no longer certain whether it had been Jed or her father who had taught her to ride, break horses, and shoot a gun.

In the years since her father's death, Jessie had become an able businesswoman and a just boss, but she depended greatly on Jed's common sense and easy way of handling the men who worked on her ranch. Jessie took an active hand in the actual physical running of the ranch, and her presence at roundups, brandings, and auctions was accepted without question. Most of the day-to-day affairs, however, were left to Jed, whom she trusted completely. Jed, in turn, couldn't have been more proud of his own child.

"I've seen them like that before, Jess. Stubborn streak a mile wide. He'll make you a great horse if you can win him."

Laughing, Jessie led the stallion toward the barn. "I guess my stubborn streak can stand up to his."

It was cool in the dark barn, and the smell of fresh hay was clean and sweet. Jessie removed the tack and gave Rory a brisk rubdown. There was dirt caked on her face and clothes, and a deep scratch across her right cheek. She would ache later when the bruised muscles stiffened.

Her blond hair was collar length, thick and rich, and she wore it pulled back at her neck with a wide dark ribbon. She was not vain about her physical appearance; in fact, she rarely considered it, and she wore her hair shorter than was fashionable because it was practical. She couldn't very well work with it always in her way.

"I was hoping to bring you into town for the roundup to show you off," she admonished the horse as she worked the dust from his coat with a stiff wire brush. "You'll make a great stud and father fine foals, if you don't turn out to be too wild. People don't want horses they can't ride, you know."

Her voice belied her criticism. She admired his spirit, and she wouldn't break him down if she couldn't eventually tame him with her persistence. "Guess you'll have to sit this one out."

For almost a week every year in the late spring, New Hope was the center of a huge auction where she put her animals up against those of the best ranches in the territory to buy, sell, and trade. It was always an exciting time, and she would be working day and night to purchase animals that would improve her stock and collect her profits from those she had bred and sold. Doing well at the roundup was a necessity if her ranch was to survive. She, Jed, and most of the hands would drive the horses down early on the first morning for weighing and registering. Then she would be free to look over the other stock being offered and make arrangements with fellow ranchers for sales or stud services.

Jessie had been a part of this process for as long as she could remember. Most of the ranchers had grown used to seeing little Jessie at Tom Forbes' side every year at roundup, and after Tom was killed, it was natural for Jessie to continue. She had earned a reputation as a good breeder and an honest trader. The fact that she was a woman was somehow never an issue, perhaps because she had always been there. Men who wouldn't let their daughters ride astride found nothing unusual in Jessie Forbes riding herd on her own stock or striking a business deal. Jessie was just Jessie.

Straightening up carefully, she grimaced at the ache in her

lower back. She stretched her long, slender trunk and slapped the horse's rump. "Go on, get in there. You can eat now. I'd better get moving, or I'll be too stiff to ride in the morning."

Slowly, she made her way across the yard toward the sprawling wood and stone house that had always been her home. Her father had built it to last when he had first staked his claim, well before she was born. It was of simple design, with a kitchen, pantry, parlor, and sitting room downstairs. They had never entertained anyone other than men who came to do business, and the sitting room had become her father's office. This was the room that Jessie preferred.

The heavy leather chairs, gun racks, and shelves of books were strangely restful. A sitting room with lace-covered couches and fine glassware would only have made her nervous. She often read for a few hours at night before the fire in her library, choosing from the collection of books that had been her father's. When she made her semi-annual trip into Bannack, the territorial capital, for the supplies she could not get closer to home, she always tried to find something new to add.

Her days were full, and she was rarely lonely. On the infrequent evenings when a strange melancholy stole over her, she had only to stand on the porch, looking out on the land that sustained her, and she would find her peace.

⌘ ❖ ♦ ❖ ♦ ❖ ♦ ⌘

"Mr. Schroeder?" Kate asked as her father and his friend joined the women in the parlor following an after-dinner cigar out on the porch. "Please tell us about the roundup tomorrow."

After only a month in her new home, Kate felt as if she had always lived there. She still had much to learn about everyday life without the comforts that she had been used to, but she viewed each new challenge as a test of her own ability. She looked happy, and she was.

"Humph. Just an excuse for those cowboys to come into town and tear the place up," Hannah grumbled as she reached for her sewing.

Thaddeus laughed, casting his wife an affectionate glance.

"Don't you go listening to Hannah, now, Kate. The spring roundup is one of the biggest events in this town. Ranchers and drovers come from hundreds of miles, and the place fills up, to be sure. The hotel can't handle 'em all, and the saloon, well..." He glanced at his wife. "I guess things do get a little wild at times, but they're a good-natured bunch."

"Heavens, is it safe to go out?" Martha asked with concern. She pictured hordes of men riding roughshod through the streets.

"Now, Martha," Martin began, aware that his wife still found the rough western ways unsettling.

"It's not like it used to be, Martha," Thaddeus replied kindly. "The whole town gets involved. There'll be a big cele-bration the last day of the auction, over at the church. Most of the women prepare food and there's a dance. My Hannah is known for her pies over the whole territory."

Hannah blushed and shushed him.

"I am so looking forward to it," Kate said with real enthusi-asm. This certainly sounded much more interesting than the afternoons she recalled, sitting in a somber parlor discussing topics of no consequence with would-be suitors, who didn't appear to care what her thoughts might be. She was relieved to have left that behind, if only temporarily.

"Will all the ranchers be there?" Kate continued, thinking about one rancher in particular. As different as the young women of New Hope might be from Kate's friends in Boston, in one way they were very much the same. They still spent their lives learn-ing to be wives. Kate appreciated the way these women toiled so their families might survive in a harsh, unforgiving land, but as she dutifully spent time with Hannah Schroeder learning how to preserve meat without ice or the best way to fashion pillow slips from old dresses, she thought about Jessie Forbes. Jessie owned property and went about town doing business unescorted, a dar-ing possibility of which Kate had never even conceived. The quiet, self-possessed rancher was unlike any other woman Kate had ever met, and she wanted to see her again.

"That's right; every rancher in the territory will be here," Thaddeus Schroeder confirmed.

Kate looked to her father. "I'd like to watch the auction

tomorrow. Where will it be?"

"I guess it's safe enough, isn't it?" Martin asked of Thaddeus, ignoring the concerned expression on his wife's face.

Thaddeus nodded. "Why of course, Kate. I'll have John Emory take you over in the morning to see where the stock will be corralled. Some of the nearby ranchers will be here by then."

Kate smiled slightly. "That's just what I was hoping."

Chapter
4

"Father didn't say you'd be wanting to tote half the house out here with us," John grumbled good-humoredly. He grunted slightly as he shifted the heavy cases he carried in both hands. It was a common sight to see young John Schroeder escorting the pretty Beecher girl about town, and people greeted them with friendly hellos as they passed.

"Oh, John." Kate laughed and looked up at him fondly. "How could I miss this opportunity to make photographs?"

He had seen traveling photographers before, and his father had several examples of their craft hanging in the newspaper office, but he had never seen a photograph made. He had also never seen a woman do anything of the kind. Secretly, he was astonished that Kate could make those pictures he had seen at the Beecher house. She tried to explain the process to him, saying it was quite simple, but he could not grasp it. The mystery of it only served to elevate Kate in his eyes.

"Are you sure about all this?" he asked a bit suspiciously. In one of the cases he could hear liquid sloshing.

"Yes," she assured him. "This was my father's equipment, and I've helped him make photographs since I was a little girl. He grew tired of it, but I never have. It was the *one* thing I would not leave behind." She looked around her at the sharply rising hills and the expanse of endless sky and thought that she had never seen country more beautiful. "I can't wait to capture just a little of this on the plates."

"Humph. Just a roundup, like all the others," he complained, but he thought himself the most fortunate man in town and would gladly have carried the damn cases all day. "Say, why don't we go over under those trees. You can see the auction stand and the corrals across the yard."

Kate nodded her approval. Already, she was amazed at the number of people filling the street. There was a contagious excitement in the air, borne on the sounds of men shouting and agitated livestock snorting and whinnying. She was captivated by the sight of the large animals milling about in the pens, huge masses of restless power. The immediacy and urgency of life in this untamed place was thrilling.

The cowboys who tended the corrals leaned up against fences or trees, talking quietly in groups, sharing a smoke. They certainly didn't look wild to Kate. She scanned the crowd, looking for Jessie Forbes' distinctive figure, but was disappointed not to find the rancher among the early arrivals.

Contenting herself with photographing the surrounding activity, she was soon lost in her work. She exposed several plates, anxious to depict the anticipation of the waiting stands before the auction began. It was a time-consuming process because she had to fix the wet plates almost immediately or the surface would dry and lose the image she had so carefully sought. She was just about to expose her last plate when she heard John at her elbow.

"Miss Kate, you'd better let me get that contraption out of here," he said urgently. "There's a herd coming this way, and you're going to be mighty close."

"Just fifteen more seconds, John," Kate answered calmly. This was a good exposure, perhaps the best that morning, and she was not going to ruin it. It took her nearly an hour to prepare the mixture of egg precipitate and chemicals that coated the plates and longer still to develop each one into a finished image.

"Please, Miss Kate!" John shouted, tugging at her sleeve.

Under the camera cloth, Kate heard muffled shouts to her

right and felt a tremble in her camera support. Even as the sound of thundering hoof-beats grew closer, she couldn't imagine what the fuss was about.

"Three, two, one..." she whispered, closing the shutter and lifting the cloth from her shoulders. "Oh!" she cried, grasping John's arm in stunned alarm.

Not fifty feet away, dozens of horses were streaming into an open pen as cowboys rode back and forth along the outskirts of the herd, trying to direct the fast moving animals into the corrals. Men surrounded her, shouting and waving their hats. A haze of dust billowed upward, engulfing her, and Kate stumbled backwards to the shelter of the trees, coughing and wiping dirt from her eyes. John had the presence of mind to drag her camera back with him as he joined her. He shouted something to her, but his words were lost in the uproar of bellowing men and rampaging horses.

Through eyes streaming with tears, Kate made out a dozen men herding the stragglers into the pen. The leader of the group leaned down from his saddle to swing the corral gate shut. With a quick flick of the horse's head, he turned toward Kate and John and approached at a gallop.

Kate edged a little closer to John as the horse and rider drew down upon them, kicking up clouds of dirt anew. She was sure that they were about to be trampled. When the charging horse was only a few feet away, or so it seemed to Kate, she saw the rider rise up out of the seat and dismount on the run. Before she could catch her breath, the cowboy, caked in dirt from head to toe, grabbed John Schroeder by the shirtfront.

"Damn it, John! What's got into you, letting her get that close to the pens? If a stray had got loose from that bunch, it could have run her down. I've a good mind to throw you into that corral over there and let my horses stomp some sense into you."

Jessie Forbes was so mad she couldn't see straight. It was only because John Schroeder was a boy she liked that she didn't do more damage than a sound shaking. She forced herself to let him go, turning to ask Kate, "Are you all right, Miss Beecher?"

Jessie's heart was still pounding with the sudden surge of panic she had experienced seeing Kate in the road as she led her herd down the main street into town. As the horses in the lead had already spread out across the entire width of the road, Jessie barely had time to direct the wranglers between Kate and the galloping steeds. Another minute and Kate would have been under their hooves.

Kate stared open-mouthed, more surprised by Jessie's sudden appearance than the previous threat of unbridled charging horses. The rancher's face was streaked with dirt, and there was an angry welt running across her right cheek. Her shirt was plastered to her chest with sweat. She stood with her hands curled around the belt of her wide, black holster, her long legs planted a little apart. Kate thought Jessie's hands trembled as they clenched the leather.

"It wasn't his fault," Kate croaked, her throat parched and sore from the dust.

Finally remembering to sweep off her hat, Jessie forced a smile through her anger. "Now that's where you're wrong, Miss Beecher. It *is* right well his fault. He should have looked after you, being a newcomer. He knows what to expect around here on roundup day."

John nodded in agreement, having forgotten his initial scare when Jessie had grabbed him. He'd thought for a minute there that he was in for a whupping and suspected he probably deserved one. "You're right, Jessie. She could have gotten—"

"Now just one minute," Kate interrupted hotly, her dark eyes blazing. "I am not a helpless child, you know. I have two legs, and I could have moved if I had wanted. I certainly do not need either one of you deciding where I should stand."

Jessie and John stared at her wordlessly, and Kate stared back, her face flushed. She saw a grin flicker across Jessie's fine mouth, and her anger slowly ebbed. Then Jessie tilted her head back and laughed, and, after a second, Kate joined her. John gaped at them as if they had both taken leave of their senses.

Jessie's tense body relaxed, and she smiled down at Kate. "What was that thing you had out there anyhow?"

"A camera. I was trying to capture the feeling of this whole thing," Kate answered, taking in the street and the corrals with a sweep of her arm.

"Well, you almost got more of a feel for it than you bargained on, Miss Beecher."

"Kate," Kate said softly.

Jessie looked at her intently, her eyes sparkling. "Kate."

"You've hurt yourself," Kate said, studying Jessie with a worried expression.

"What?" Jessie replied, confused.

Kate's soft hand brushed gently across Jessie's face, touching the swollen cheek. Jessie blushed and turned her head away.

"Oh, that's nothing. I've been having a running battle with a new stallion I had the misfortune of acquiring. He and I don't see eye to eye on which one of us is the boss just yet."

"I find that hard to believe," Kate answered steadily, her dark eyes fixed on the rancher's face. Jessie impressed her as the most capable woman she could imagine.

Jessie wasn't sure why Kate's words stirred a flutter in her chest, but she cleared her throat and turned to John. "I've got to see to my horses, John. You make sure you take care of Kate, now."

"I will, Jessie," John mumbled contritely.

Kate lightly placed her hand on Jessie's sleeve and asked boldly, "Would you show me your animals later?"

Jessie's body tensed. Damn if her arm didn't shake where Kate touched her. "Well, they're just horses, you know. Nothing special."

"Yes, but I'd like to see them," Kate insisted. She *did* want to know more about the roundup, but mostly, she wanted an excuse to see more of this tough but strangely gentle woman.

"All right then." Jessie relented, surprised by Kate's request. It wasn't the sort of thing to which most women took a liking. "I'll be busy most of the morning with the weighing. If you're here this afternoon, I'll be happy to show you."

Kate smiled softly. "I'll be here."

She watched as Jessie mounted and rode quickly back to the corral, calling to her men as she went. Kate thought Jessie was quite the most dashing figure of a cowboy.

Chapter
5

Jessie worked steadily the rest of the morning in a make-shift shed by the auction stands, registering her stock and seeing to the hands. As she paid her men their wages, she knew full well that they'd likely spend a large share of it during the next week. Most of them would come straggling back to the ranch when their money was gone, ready to sign on for another year. A few would answer the call of wanderlust, eager to discover what was over the next mountain ridge, and never pass this way again.

The life was a hard one, and she didn't begrudge her men their pleasures. She enjoyed a good hand of cards herself and more often than not came away a winner. It was no secret that the saloon offered more than gaming tables and good whiskey, too. Everyone in town knew that the women who lived upstairs in the hotel earned their living by befriending the cowboys who passed through. It was as much a part of life as anything else, and Jessie accepted that as uncritically as her men accepted her.

"Don't spend it all tonight, Sam," she said as she handed the draft to her lead trail man.

"No, ma'am," he exclaimed, grinning sheepishly.

"You make sure the boys don't cause trouble this week. I don't want it said the Forbes boys were running wild."

"I'll see to it, Miss Jessie," the big man replied earnestly.

There were some transients among their group, but most had been with Jessie through more than one roundup, and all of them were proud to work for her. She was fair and paid top wages. Her ability to rope and ride with the best of them had earned her their respect and loyalty.

"You can tell the boys the week is theirs, but I expect you all to ride out of here with me come next Monday," she said, pushing her chair back from the rickety wooden table and gathering her account papers.

Sam grinned down at her. "They'll be pleased to hear that, ma'am. It's been a long time between roundups."

Jessie sighed, running a weary hand over her face. "I know it, Sam. But we've a fine herd to show for it, and I'm right pleased with all of you."

Sam flushed, happy with the compliment. He tipped his hat and turned to leave, almost bumping into Kate. "Sorry, Miss," he said as he walked away.

"Am I early?" Kate asked as she approached the table, smiling.

Jessie smiled back, folding her papers and slipping them into the saddlebag by her side. "No, I've just finished." Standing, she rubbed her face again ruefully and laughed. "If you'll give me a bit though, I'll get washed up. I feel like one of my horses just now—rode hard and put up wet."

Kate stared at her, struggling for the meaning of the expression, but one look at Jessie told the story. She was still dusty from the trail, and there were circles shadowing her dark blue eyes. She was clearly exhausted.

"How long has it been since you've been to bed?" Kate asked.

Jessie shrugged. "It takes the better part of a month to get the herd down from the high country where they winter, then foal in the spring. Always stragglers getting lost up some canyon or other. It takes every able body on the ranch to bring 'em in. Not many of us slept more than a few hours in a row for a while."

"We could do this another time," Kate offered, trying to hide her disappointment. She had hurried through dinner preparations with her mother so that she might have the rest of the day free to spend with Jessie.

"Oh, no." Jessie laughed again. "No way am I going to be tucked abed somewhere when I could be making a deal, or," she finished shyly, "taking a walk for no other reason than the fun of it."

Kate blushed, unaccountably pleased. "Are you staying at the hotel then?"

"Yes. Most everybody's got a room there for the week," she said as they turned toward town. She glanced at the clear blue sky, aware for the first time what an unusually fine day it was. "I won't be long. Where do you want me to meet you?"

"I'll walk you to the hotel, if you don't mind," Kate replied, suddenly afraid that Jessie might change her mind after all.

"I'd enjoy the company," Jessie said quietly, surprised that it was true. She was used to going long stretches without talking to anyone, except maybe Jed about some problem at the ranch. The idea of walking in the warm afternoon sun with Kate Beecher seemed more than pleasant. "You folks all settled?"

"I'm not sure that I'd call it 'settled' exactly," Kate said with a laugh as they strolled through the town toward the hotel, which was clearly the center of activity. "My father is quite beside himself with pleasure, but it's hard for my mother. The simple things we took for granted, like household items and ready-made clothes, are rarities here. Hannah Schroeder has been a great help, and I think I'm beginning to master the basics, but it's much different than I expected."

Jessie had never given such things much thought. Life at the ranch was simple. What they couldn't buy in the way of tools or goods, they made or went without. She didn't need more than the clothes she worked in. Game was plentiful on the range, and enough of her neighbors farmed that she could buy food staples for herself and her men locally. "I imagine it feels pretty uncivilized out here to you," she mused.

"No," Kate replied quietly, "it feels free."

Jessie heard the wistful tone in Kate's voice and tried to envision another life, a life where she wasn't free to come and go as she pleased, where she wasn't free to make her own choices. She couldn't imagine it.

They walked on in companionable silence the short distance to the hotel. Cowboys in groups and pairs straggled in and out of the saloon on the first floor, shouting to friends they had not seen for months. Many waved or called to Jessie, who nodded back. Piano music floated through the open doors, providing a festive background to the general cacophony.

"There's a stairway around back here," Jessie said, leading the way down the narrow alley between the hotel and the land office. "That's no place for you in there."

"And you?" Kate questioned, amused at Jessie's protective attitude but touched by it, too.

"Oh, that's different. I've ridden with most of those men and played cards with more than a few," she replied straightforwardly. "Had to carry a couple of 'em home on more than one occasion. But no lady would want to go in there. Roundup time is a little crazy."

"I see," Kate said gravely.

Jessie caught the faint mocking tone in Kate's voice and saw the shadow of a smile flicker across Kate's smooth features. "Sorry. Don't mean to be preaching at you."

Kate laughed in turn. "Come on, let's get you upstairs."

They climbed the outside wooden steps to the second floor and walked down the hallway to Jessie's room. A plain bedstead held a narrow mattress; a single bureau, with a pitcher and basin on the top, stood against one wall; and a threadbare braid rug covered part of the floor. Jessie drew the only chair up to the window so Kate would have a good view of the activities below.

"I'll just be a minute. I want to wash the dust off my face and get into some pants that don't stand up by themselves."

Kate watched as Jessie unbuckled the heavy gun strapped to her thigh and laid it casually on the bed, stripping off the leather chaps she wore over her pants as well. "Is that what you call a six-shooter?" she asked.

Jessie looked at her, poised with one foot up to pull off her boots. "Most side arms nowadays hold six bullets in the chamber. They vary a bit depending on the caliber of the bullets. That's a Colt forty-five. All the Army carries them. They call it a peacemaker, but I suspect they're foolin' about that."

"Oh, I see," Kate said, catching the sarcasm in the way Jessie said Army. "I take it you don't care for soldiers."

"I don't know as how I like or dislike 'em, really. It just gets a bit aggravating when the government sends troops who don't understand the land or the customs or the people and then tries to say they're the law."

"Have they bothered you at the ranch?" Kate asked, genuinely curious. It had never occurred to her before that people like Jessie, whose family had carved a life out of this inhospitable land, often at great sacrifice, might not welcome the representatives of a government far removed.

"They help themselves to a cow now or then," Jessie allowed. "I'd gladly give them what they want when they need food, but they don't seem to think asking is necessary."

"That probably never occurred to them," Kate remarked angrily, feeling outraged on Jessie's behalf.

"I imagine we do a lot of things different out here than back East," Jessie said quietly.

"Have you ever been to the East?" Kate turned her chair from the window, finding nothing in the streets below that interested her as much as Jessie Forbes.

Jessie walked to the sideboard and poured a basin of water. "My father said my mother would have wanted me to go for more schooling," she said, splashing her face, then dousing her head. She reached blindly for a towel and covered her face. "I hated the idea, but I was supposed to go when I was seventeen. My father was stubborn on that point."

"But you didn't?" Kate asked with interest.

Jessie stiffened slightly as she opened the valise at the end of the bed. Pulling clean but faded denim pants and an embroidered shirt from the case, she answered softly, "My father died in a stampede a month before I was supposed to go. I had to stay and run the ranch."

"Oh, I'm sorry, Jessie," Kate proclaimed quickly.

Jessie shook her head. "It's all right. That sort of thing happens out here."

Kate heard the edge of pain in Jessie's voice but said nothing. She couldn't imagine losing her father so tragically, and she knew how much it must have hurt. She didn't think Jessie could be that much older than herself, and she marveled at the young rancher's composure, thinking that she had rarely met anyone more self-assured.

Still sorting her thoughts, Kate was caught off-guard as Jessie slipped off her grimy shirt and pants. Involuntarily, she drew in a sharp breath, surprised by the thin cotton undershirt the other woman wore in place of a corset and alarmed by the large bruise covering her left thigh. "You *are* hurt!" she exclaimed without thinking.

Jessie turned, reaching for her clean pants, clearly taken unawares. She saw the direction of Kate's gaze and looked down. "Oh, that. Pretty sorry excuse for a rancher, huh?" she said with a chuckle. "Just another little present from that stallion of mine." She pulled up her pants and tucked in her shirt.

Kate was captivated by the easy way Jessie moved and the sinewy strength of her limbs. She found her heart racing and looked away, confused by the sudden fluttering in her stomach.

"You must find this town a great disappointment after Boston," Jessie continued, unaware of Kate's discomfort.

"Oh no, I love it," Kate cried, almost startling herself when she realized how true that was. "Life is so different here, and there is so much to learn. Besides, there is no one like you in Boston..." She blushed suddenly, embarrassed by her forward remark.

Jessie laughed and reached for her holster. "I don't imagine I'd fit in too well back there."

"No," Kate said softly. "No, you wouldn't. I'm glad you aren't there."

Jessie stared at her closely, held by the quiet intensity in her voice. Kate seemed quite unlike the shy young women Jessie had gone to school with in New Hope. Despite her sophistication, Kate was easy to talk to, something Jessie was surprised to discover she enjoyed.

"I'm glad I'm not there either," Jessie said with a grin, pulling on her worn leather boots. "I suppose it will take some getting used to, but I hope you'll be happy here, Kate."

"I feel as if this is where I belong," Kate answered, never

meaning it more than she did in that moment.

Jessie chuckled again and stretched, feeling wonderful all of a sudden. Her fatigue had magically vanished. "Do you still want to see those horses of mine?"

"Oh, yes."

"Come on, then," Jessie said, reaching for her hand, taking it gently. "We'd better go before it gets to be dinner time."

Kate was surprised by Jessie's careful strength and the utter tenderness of her touch. Unexpectedly, quite unable to move, she sat staring up at Jessie, whose eyes suddenly grew dark. A pulse beat visibly in the rancher's neck, just above the collar of her shirt. Kate felt her own heart beat hard against the inside of her chest. For a moment, neither of them spoke. Kate swallowed, aware of the faint tremor in Jessie's fingers that matched her own.

"Yes," Kate whispered as they both drew shyly away at the same time. She rose, trying to ignore the slight unsteadiness in her limbs. "We should go."

Chapter
6

Kate and Jessie spent the rest of the afternoon wandering about the auction pens. Jessie pointed out her herd and explained some of its history to her interested companion.

"Our stock is pure Appaloosa—Plains Indian bred—with a little wild mustang thrown in to make 'em tough. My father was one of the first ranchers in this area. He was on his way to the Oregon territory with all the other fools looking for gold when my mother convinced him that land was where the real value lay, or so he told it."

Jessie leaned a foot up on the rail and dangled her forearms over the top of the corral, watching one particularly frisky colt kick up his heels. "Back then, the Indians and the settlers got along pretty well, before the Indians started getting crowded out of their land. They traded freely with the first settlers, including bartering their horses for supplies that the expeditions brought. My father found himself a couple of hands as crazy as him, and he started chasing down the wild horses to build our line. There were no reservations on the northern plains either. As long as he stayed clear of the Indian hunting grounds, there wasn't any problem." She frowned. "All the problems started when the damn Army started telling the Indians where they had to live." She looked quickly at Kate. "Sorry for the cussing."

Kate shook her head. "I won't faint from a word, Jessie." She had heard of the "Indian troubles," but until then it had seemed very much like the war with the South—something that didn't really affect her. Suddenly, it seemed much more important.

Questions tumbled out one after the other, and Jessie answered good-naturedly. The two young women didn't notice the sun starting to set until a brisk breeze caused Kate to shiver slightly and pull her shawl tightly about her.

Looking up at the sky, Jessie was amazed that she had lost track of time. That was something she never did. "Lord, Kate. It's later than I thought. You should be getting back."

Kate shook her head in protest. "Oh no. There's so much I want to know. Plus," she added impulsively, "I'm having too much fun."

Jessie laughed, twirling her hat between her long, graceful fingers. "So am I, but won't your parents worry?"

"Probably," Kate sighed. "Despite the fact that I'm eighteen and quite capable of looking after myself."

"I expect you are," Jessie said seriously, "but this isn't Boston, Kate. Young women can't be out wandering after dark. I'll take you home."

"And I suppose you're quite safe?" Kate retorted, a storm threatening in her eyes. She would not have Jessie thinking of her as a child.

Jessie stared at her, confused by her sudden anger. "Kate," she said softly, "I'm not like you. There isn't a man in this town who would try to take advantage of me."

Kate blushed, understanding her meaning and feeling foolish for not realizing that Jessie had only been thinking of her safety. It had nothing to do with her age and much more to do with the gun on Jessie's thigh.

"I'm sorry," Kate said swiftly.

Jessie shook her head. "No need. Now let's get you home. Where is it?"

"At the other end of town, near the south fork."

Walking through town, they passed townspeople making their way home and cowboys lounging on the sidewalks. With

Jessie striding confidently beside her, Kate realized that she had never felt so free, and yet so secure.

As they approached the gate in front of Kate's home, Jessie stopped. "I'll say goodnight now, Kate," she said quietly.

"Come in for dinner, please," Kate said suddenly, placing her hand on Jessie's arm. "It's the least I can do after you walked all this way."

The rancher looked away, uncomfortable. "No, thank you. I've got to check on the stock anyhow. You go on in."

Kate frowned slightly and faced Jessie squarely. "I had a wonderful time, Jessie. Thank you."

Jessie smiled, her eyes meeting Kate's. "No need to thank me for something I enjoyed more than anything I can recall in a long time."

It was Kate's turn to smile. She stood on the porch for long minutes until Jessie's retreating form blended into the night.

Chapter
7

"Kate!" Martha cried as her daughter came hurriedly through the door. "Where have you been? It's late and we were worried sick." She grabbed Kate by the shoulders and peered at her intently. "I was about to send your father out to search for you."

"For heaven's sake, Martha," Martin exclaimed. "Let the girl talk."

"I was down at the auction grounds. You knew that," Kate answered, her thoughts still on her afternoon with Jessie. "And it's not even dark yet."

"I know I've said this is a safe town, but this week especially," Martin began gently, "it's not safe for a young girl out alone at this hour."

"I was *not* alone," Kate replied, more forcefully than she had intended. Only moments ago, she had experienced an independence she'd never imagined, simply spending an afternoon as she chose, walking with a woman she admired. Now her parents acted as if she weren't capable of basic good judgment. She rankled under their well-meaning restraints. "I was with a friend and quite safe."

"And who *was* that young man who brought you home?" Martha queried archly.

Kate flushed a deep scarlet, her black eyes flashing against her pale skin. For a moment, she was too angry to speak.

"That was *not* a young man," she asserted indignantly. "That was Jessie Forbes. She's a rancher from north of town." Uncertain why she did, Kate felt instantly protective of Jessie. *Silly,* she thought, *because if anyone doesn't need protecting, it's Jessie Forbes.* Still, she faced her mother with a defiant glint in her eye.

"A woman!" Martha declared, appalled.

Martin relaxed perceptibly and chuckled. "Kate couldn't have been with anyone safer, my dear. Jessie Forbes is an extremely capable young woman. I met her at the newspaper office some weeks ago. As Kate said, she runs a ranch—apparently quite successfully. She's bright and has a sound head on her shoulders."

Martha turned from daughter to husband, a shocked expression on her face. "I saw this young woman, Martin, and it's a...a...a *disgrace*. She was wearing pants!"

"Well goodness, Martha. This isn't Boston. You could hardly expect her to tend her herd in a dress," Martin replied easily. "Out here women dress more practically."

"Practically?" Martha, who even now would not consider wearing the popular bloomer, was scandalized. She looked with concern at Kate, who continued to look rebellious. "I hope this isn't the kind of thing that you find admirable. No decent woman would be found dressed like that in public. And I do believe she was wearing a gun."

"Actually, it's a Colt forty-five peacemaker, Mother," Kate announced, dropping her shawl on a chair and walking to her father. She took his arm, avoiding her mother's astounded stare. "Shall we have dinner?"

⌘ ❖ ♦ ❖ ♦ ❖ ♦ ⌘

Jessie awakened shortly after nine that night, ravenous. After checking her stock, she'd returned to her room and stretched out on the bed, meaning only to close her eyes for a moment. She'd thought back to the afternoon and the pleasure she had drawn from Kate's company. With the memory of Kate's quick smile playing through her mind, she had drifted off to sleep.

Once awake, she washed quickly, threw on a leather vest over her shirt, and went in search of food. In the mood for a thick steak and some fried potatoes, she ate alone in the nearly deserted hotel dining room and then ambled into the saloon. The din of male voices was considerable, and the air was ripe with the odor of horses, well-worked men, and rivers of whiskey. She pushed her way through the crowd to the end of the bar, away from the bulk of the cowboys and the occasional dancehall girl.

"Evening, Frank. Guess business is good, huh?" she greeted the bartender.

"Jessie Forbes!" shouted the portly bewhiskered man behind the long, scarred bar. "Good to see you. Yep, there's quite a crowd here tonight. Can I get you something?"

"I think a brandy," she replied, fishing a coin from her levis.

Drink in hand, she turned to watch the room, tipping her glass now and then when someone called a greeting. Those who didn't know her personally had heard of her from others. She did not feel strange in the room full of men, because, in many ways, she was like them. She lived and worked on the same land as they, sweated the same on a hard day's ride, and bled just as easily when a horse kicked a stone her way or a jerked rope burned a raw gash across her palm. She gave it no more thought than she did to what the next day would bring. She was a rancher; that was her life.

A man moved close to her in the press of bodies growing denser near the bar. "Cards, Jess?"

Jessie turned toward him, her face lighting with pleasure. "Hank Trilby. How are you? And how are things at your ranch?"

"I brought my first herd down today, Jess, and it's a fine bunch." The tall, dark-haired cowboy grinned with pride. "Hope you take a look at them tomorrow."

Hank had been with her father before Tom Forbes' death and had stayed on for a year or two after Jessie took over the ranch. When he had a chance to buy into a spread nearby, Jessie had willingly backed him. She had not been wrong. Hank owned the ranch now and was doing well.

"I'll do that, Hank. I've been looking for a few new mares. Did I hear you say cards?"

Hank laughed, pointing to a table at one side of the room where four men sat dealing cards. "We've been waiting for an easy mark," he teased.

Jessie laughed, her eyes twinkling. "Haven't you got enough there already?"

⌘ ❖ ♦ ❖ ♦ ❖ ♦ ⌘

Well after midnight, Jessie pushed her chair back and tossed her cards down. "That's it, boys. If I stay any longer I'll be selling next year's herd."

Several men laughed, knowing that, if anything, she was slightly ahead. As she rose from the table, a soft voice at her elbow murmured, "Hello, Montana."

Jessie turned, her gaze falling on a woman with long blond hair that cascaded thickly over bare, milk-pale shoulders. Her dress was emerald green, low cut and close fitting, with a constraining bodice that boldly lifted her breasts to the verge of immodesty and beyond.

"Why, hello, Mae," Jessie replied warmly. "I'm about ready to turn in, but would you like to have a brandy with me first? You can catch me up on all the news."

Mae gave a deep-throated chuckle and rested her well-kept hand against Jessie's sturdy shoulder. "You can have a brandy, Montana. I'll have a whiskey, thanks."

Jessie smiled and made a path for them to the bar. As she placed Mae's drink down, Jessie recalled the first time they had met. It must have been her first roundup after her father had died. She had been barely eighteen and had come looking for Jed in the saloon one night when their best brood mare had gone down with colic out in the stockyard.

The saloon was more crowded than ever. As she searched the room for her men, a big, burly Texan, a stranger, grabbed her roughly from behind.

"Now looky here, will you, boys? Just take a gander at what wandered in. Isn't she a fine one, though, and wearing a side arm, too!" He laughed drunkenly and pulled her hat off. Then he put that hand under her chin while the other still grasped her arm.

Out of the corner of her eye, Jessie saw Jed with several others heading toward her, blood in their eyes. In a minute, there would be a brawling fight, or worse. She stood very still and raised one hand slightly, waving her men away. Jed stopped, his body tense, and signaled to the others to wait, but his eyes never left Jessie's face.

Pulling her hat from the Texan's grasp, she stepped back, freeing her other arm as she did so. Slowly, with careful deliberation, she replaced her hat and quietly regarded the leering cowboy.

"I'm Jessie Forbes. You must be new around here or else you'd know that. I don't believe I know your name. I'm here looking for my men, and I'd appreciate it if you'd let me through." She spoke quietly, but her words carried to those nearest her. Several men turned a watchful eye on the cowboy. The air crackled with tension.

"Oh, you'd like to get by, would you?" he mocked, swaying slightly and making another grab for her. *"How would you like to come upstairs with me instead? Might be I could show you a good time."*

Jessie sidestepped quickly and remained facing him. *"Mister, I wouldn't take any pleasure in killing you, but you're wearing out my patience. These fellas here are all trying to enjoy this roundup, and so am I. Nobody wants trouble. Now, I don't want to have my men get all busted up trying to make you be reasonable, so if you don't go off somewhere and let me be, I'm gonna have to shoot you myself."* She spoke quietly and hadn't made any move toward her gun, but several cowboys nearby drew sharp breaths and pushed quickly out of the way.

The stranger laughed hoarsely, his eyes flickering to the faces around him. None were friendly.

"You think you can take me?" he jeered, licking his lips, which were suddenly dry.

"I can, but I'd rather not." Her voice was soft, but every man in the room heard her.

He looked at the deadly calm in her eyes and dropped his gaze. "I ain't never shot no woman, and you ain't gonna be the first," he muttered, turning slowly away.

As quickly as it had begun, it was over, but Jessie had won her rightful place in the mind of every man present. As Jessie made her way through the crowd, a woman approached, stopping her with a hand on her arm. Jessie remembered that her eyes had been as green as spring grass, deep and warm.

"I want to thank you for keeping these damn fools from tearing up this place. I'm afraid some of my girls would have been hurt. Mind you, I think you're daft."

That had happened six roundups ago, and over the years since, she and Mae had become friends. Whenever Jessie was in town, she made it a point to stop in the saloon to say hello or buy Mae a drink after the last of the cowhands had staggered off at the end of the night. Their friendship was an unconscious appreciation between two women who were often misunderstood, and Jessie had learned to value their moments together. She could talk to Mae in a way that she could to no one else, not even Jed.

"Hey, Montana, what are you dreaming about?" Mae asked as she circled her glass over the top of the bar, watching the dark liquid swirl close to the brim.

Jessie smiled at the woman pressed close against her side. Mae's head barely reached her shoulder, and Jessie had to lean down to make herself heard. "I was remembering that first night when I met you."

"Oh Lord, that was a sight." Mae laughed, downing the whiskey shot in one practiced flick of her wrist. "You and that cowboy in a standoff. Would you have really shot that fella?"

Jessie grinned suddenly. "I don't know. I hadn't thought about it yet." She laughed at the look of dismay on her companion's face. "How are you, Mae? It seems like an age since we've talked."

"Oh, a little older, Jess, but still holding up. Haven't seen you around too much these last few months. Not forgetting old friends, are you?" Mae searched Jessie's face, realizing once again how fine looking she was. *Too handsome for a woman, but too pleasing to the eye for a man.*

Jessie smiled at her fondly and shook her head. "Not you, Mae. I couldn't forget you."

Mae colored slightly and gazed at their reflections in the mirror behind the bar, choosing her words carefully. "Say, Montana, who was that young woman I saw you strolling through town with today? Don't think I know her."

Jessie turned startled eyes on Mae. "Why, her name is Kate Beecher, Mae. She and her family just moved here from Boston. I didn't see you. Why didn't you call out?"

"Oh, I was busy doing something as I recollect. An Easterner, you say?" She sounded wary.

"What's the matter, Mae?" Jessie asked, surprised by the suspicion in her voice.

Mae forced a laugh and looked up at Jessie, saying lightly, "Why nothing, Jess. It's just that you have to remember those Easterners are flighty. They come out here and everything is new and different, and they fall in love with the sparkle of it. Only, after a while, they get tired of it and throw it all away like a worn-out shoe."

Jessie stared at Mae, trying to understand what she was talking about. She was still thinking about it later that night when she fell tiredly into bed.

Chapter
8

Kate was at the auction as early as she could manage the next morning, having recruited John Schroeder to carry her camera and equipment once again. This time she chose a spot that wasn't directly in the path of careening livestock.

Women from town had set up tables under a grove of trees just beyond the stockyards and were providing refreshments and sandwiches for the hordes of men congregating in front of the stands. Children raced about while worried mothers followed frantically behind them. And the ranchers and cowboys kept coming, driving herds into town day and night. The number of men in town had swelled during the night, and the sound of boisterous revelry had filled the streets well after midnight the night before.

Kate had lain awake for hours, listening to the echoes of laughter on the night air, thinking about her day. She could not recall a time that she had ever enjoyed more. She could have talked with Jessie Forbes for hours, and she so wanted the chance to see her again. When she had announced at breakfast that she was planning on returning to the auction, Kate's mother objected.

"What could possibly interest you in that place?" Martha

asked in exasperation. "Nothing but dirt, animals, and rough men."

"Everything," Kate excitedly replied. "There is so much to see, and so many things to learn."

"And what about your plans to help Hannah with the spinning today?"

Kate knew that her mother considered this, at least, a useful skill. Despite the fact that the dry goods store stocked sewing material and even some apparel brought by wagon from the East, it was clear that most clothing and household linens were going to need to be fashioned by hand.

"I'm going to the Schroeder's as soon as the breakfast dishes are finished," Kate affirmed, knowing there were things she must learn that she had never dreamed of needing to do before. Most of the time, she welcomed the opportunity to spend time with Hannah and some of the other women, but her heart wasn't in it today. Not when a mile away, the streets teemed with excitement.

"Roundup only comes once a year, Martha," Martin offered, seeing the disappointment in Kate's face. He was as distracted by all the goings-on as his daughter, but he at least had the excuse of gathering information for the paper to explain his attendance at the events. "I'm sure that Mrs. Schroeder won't mind Kate's absence for a few days. I'll walk Kate over there myself just to make sure."

As anticipated, Hannah more than understood. She was packing lunches when Martin and Kate arrived, explaining that she had volunteered to watch one of the food tables. When Kate promised to help her later that day, Hannah shooed her off with John in tow, saying, "You two go on then. I'm 'most done here, and I've seen plenty of roundups. I don't mind missing a few hours of this one."

So by late morning, Kate was eagerly searching the crowds for a sign of Jessie Forbes. She was beginning to despair as she wended her way through throngs of men, down one dusty aisle after another, passing corral after corral of animals that all looked alike on every side. The cowboys looked all of a kind, too. Broad-brimmed hats, vests over faded cotton shirts, dusty levis, and the ever-present leather chaps. Most had smudges of trail dirt on their faces, too, rendering them nearly interchangeable. Until Kate saw her.

Then she wondered how she had ever mistaken her for one of the cowboys just a few weeks before. Jessie stood talking with a burly fellow, her face in profile to Kate. Even with the brim of her hat tipped down, throwing shadows over her eyes, Jessie's subtle grace was apparent. She was lean and taut, much like some of the younger men, but the gentle arch of her neck and the elegant curve of her jaw were inherently beautiful in a way that even the handsomest youth was not.

Jessie loosely clasped her gun belt in a pose she recognized, and Kate studied those intriguing hands, fixing on the long, slender fingers. She remembered the careful way Jessie had held her hand the previous afternoon in the hotel, and her heart tripped a beat, her stomach making a sudden turn at the same time. she caught her breath, feeling suddenly, unaccountably, warm.

At that moment, Jessie turned and looked her way. She smiled, and Kate smiled back, wondering at the rush of happiness that winged to her on that glorious smile. Jessie said something to the man she was with and hurried to Kate's side.

"Why, Kate, I didn't expect to see you here again today." She surveyed the nearby crowd. "Are you alone?"

"John Emory walked me down," Kate replied. "He's off with one of the wranglers just now."

Jessie grinned. "That boy has a real itch to be a cowboy. His father has something different in mind for him, I'll wager."

"Didn't yours?" Kate asked as they walked back towards the main arena where the auctioning was about to begin. Her own parents had allowed her far more leniency than many of her girlfriends had enjoyed, letting her pursue her interest in photography, history, literature, and other subjects considered inappropriate for young women. But Kate couldn't imagine that Jessie's parents had approved of her working on the ranch. Even in this demanding place where women were forced by circumstance to labor in ways their eastern cousins would find unthinkable, Kate had quickly recognized that women still did not, as a rule, determine their own destiny.

For a moment, Jessie looked puzzled. "Not that he ever said. Out here, settlers' children always work the land in some way or another. The littlest ones carry water and feed the stock, and the older ones rope and ride or plow, whatever needs to be done."

"The girls, too?" Kate asked carefully, thinking of the newspaper accounts she had read of the suffragettes in New York State, who were speaking out for a woman's right to vote and even own property. It wasn't a popular concept. Her mother had declared that these gatherings were unseemly and that no woman with any sense would want to take on the problems that went along with having that kind of say in things. "*Some things are best left to men,*" Martha had said with a frown.

"Hello, Josiah," Jessie said to a man who spoke to them as they passed. "Well," she continued, "if there's work to be done, everybody does it. Boys cook, and men help with the wash if need be, and come harvest time, every able body in the house— man, woman, or child—is in the field."

"And shooting game and herding horses?" Kate persisted.

Jessie grinned again. "I've seen some women who were damn fine shots with a rifle. As to the riding, that's almost required if you're going to get anywhere further than town." She was suddenly serious. "My father taught me to be a rancher because I wanted to be. I don't remember much about my mother. She died of influenza when I was three. From the time I was small, I wanted to be like my father. Jed says I was riding before I could walk, and by the time I was seven, I had my first rifle. I liked school well enough, but I'd rather have been tending the herd out on the range. My father made me stay in school until I was fifteen, which is longer than any of the girls usually go. I'm glad now that he did."

Kate listened to the wistful tone in Jessie's voice and heard how much she missed her father. Kate ached for her loss, but she was struck, too, by Jessie's simple certainty. Jessie lived the life she loved. What an amazing thing. Kate walked along in silence, wondering why, until now, she had never though to question her own life and the path that had been preordained for her.

They stopped by the fence surrounding the main show ring,

and Jessie leaned her back against the rail, studying Kate. Kate's dark eyes were distant, a touch of sadness clouding her usually animated features. "What's bothering you, Kate?"

Kate blushed. "Nothing. I was just thinking how much I envy you."

Jessie laughed, that deep melodious sound Kate found so lovely. "I doubt that you'd envy me after a night sleeping out in the cold, up some canyon with nothing for company but wolves and mountain goats."

Kate laughed, too. "You'll have to take me some time so I can find out for myself." She hesitated, then went on boldly, "Would you? Take me up there sometime?"

"Kate," Jessie said softly. "It's rough country but a few dozen miles from here. Beautiful, but heartless. It's hard even for those of us who have done it all our lives." She hated the look of disappointment that flickered across Kate's face. "But I'd be happy to show you around my ranch. Not much to see but the bunkhouse and the cook cabin and a bunch of pens, but if you'd like—"

"Oh, I'd love that," Kate affirmed, "very much."

"Well, then, it's settled." Jessie pulled a watch from her pocket and frowned. "I'd better get along. I've got business waiting on me."

"I promised I'd help Mrs. Schroeder, too," Kate admitted reluctantly. "Good luck with the auction. I'll be thinking of you."

Jessie smiled, pleased. "Thank you, Kate."

"Goodbye, Jessie," Kate said softly as she watched her walk away, thinking that the rest of the day could hold nothing as pleasant as these last few moments.

⌘ ❖ ♦ ❖ ♦ ❖ ♦ ⌘

Kate had no chance to speak with Jessie again for the rest of the morning, although she looked for her constantly. Once, Kate spied her at the corral deep in conversation with another rancher; the next time, Jessie was leading a horse around the pen while several men looked the animal over. Kate waved to her on several occasions when she could catch her eye, and Jessie smiled back and tipped her hat.

Most of the time, Kate was too busy at the refreshment tables or with her photography to keep track of anyone. There was no resident photographer in the territory, and people were constantly stopping to ask her questions. Many were skeptical that she could actually master such a complicated process, but that didn't stop them from asking if she could take their pictures. Kate found herself promising to take family shots for a number of neighbors after roundup ended. She had been working steadily much of the afternoon and finally stopped when the direct heat of the sun made her increasingly uncomfortable. She folded the camera's legs and dragged it over to one of the nearby food stands.

"You're going to take a stroke standing out there with that black cloth over your head," Hannah warned as Kate joined her. She handed her a lemonade drink, and Kate took it gratefully.

"You might be right," she gasped, chasing the dust from her throat with the tart drink. "I've never had a chance to take photographs like this before. I don't want to miss a thing."

Hannah nodded. "I remember feeling that way, too, when we first arrived. When I wasn't scared to death, anyhow."

"What was it like?" Kate asked.

Hannah smiled wistfully. "Thaddeus thought he would be a homesteader, but one season on that damn prairie cured him of that. The winds in the summer blow hot enough to parch every blessed thing, and then in the winter, you freeze." She shook her head and moved the basket of food into a shadier spot on the table. "That land out there will kill you quick if you don't have a special love for it. And if it don't love you."

Kate immediately thought of Jessie, remembering the way she talked about her ranch, and nodded. "Some people belong to it, I imagine."

Hannah looked at her oddly, recalling Kate and Jessie Forbes strolling about that morning. She had thought then that it was a strange friendship. "Don't you be listening to the stories those darn cowboys tell. It ain't so pretty when you're hip deep in snow and starving. It's bad enough that John Emory's got stars in his eyes about wanting to be a wrangler. Don't you go getting ideas."

"Oh, don't worry," Kate said with a laugh. "I have no intention of becoming a cowboy." As to listening to the cowboy stories, she thought she could listen forever if it were Jessie telling the tale.

Chapter 9

After the third day of the roundup, Martha gave up trying to dissuade Kate from spending time at the auction stands. She contented herself with Kate's promise to keep out of the sun as much as possible.

"You'll ruin your skin," Martha warned.

Kate kissed her mother's cheek fondly and reached for the bonnet hanging on the coat tree by the door. "I'll wear it, don't fret!" she called as she hurried down the walk to the street.

She was eager to get there early, because she wanted to find Jessie before the business of the day became too hectic. She was taken with an idea that had come over her suddenly the night before and couldn't wait another minute to talk to Jessie about it. She headed straight for the area where she knew the Rising Star's livestock were corralled, searching for the rancher's distinctive form. When Kate saw her astride a great beast of a horse, she stopped to watch, standing back under the shade of a tree.

Jessie's face was all but indistinguishable under the low brim of her hat and the bandanna that covered her neck and mouth. She rode the horse hard from one end of the corral to the other, pulling back on the reins quickly several times to change direction and then leading his head in a tight circle so that his body nearly twisted on itself. He was powerfully built and gleamed black in the bright sunlight, a glorious mass of muscle and might.

It was the sight of Jessie, though, commanding him with the subtlest turn of her hands and the swift kick of her heels against his huge sides that captivated Kate. She stared at the way Jessie's thighs lifted slightly from the sweat-stained saddle as she leaned forward over his arching neck, urging him to run with the sheer force of her own will. Kate's breath quickened, and she was suddenly flushed, even though the air was still cool. Her heart hammered, and she bit her lip to still its trembling. She had never felt anything like this twisting, falling sensation in her belly before, and she would have been frightened if it hadn't been so terribly pleasant at the same time. She leaned against the tree, welcoming its sturdy pressure against her back and struggled to steady her shaking legs. Maybe Hannah was right. Maybe she *was* suffering from heat stroke.

⌘ ❖ ◆ ❖ ◆ ❖ ◆ ⌘

Jessie swung one leg down from the saddle, dropped easily to the ground, and walked to the fence with the reins in one hand. The horse followed, snorting noisily from his run.

"He's a dandy, Jed," she announced to her foreman. "He'd be a great line horse. He's got good legs and he never tires. I'm for buying him."

Jed nodded, chewing thoughtfully on a plug of tobacco. "If we could get us a mare or two like him, we'd have a solid start of a working brood line."

She slapped her hat against her legs, causing great clouds of dust to rise from her chaps, then wiped her sleeve across her face, her expression distant. "The railroads won't come this far north for a lot of years, and we'd have plenty of market for working horses with the stagecoaches running through here. I say we do it."

"Yep. Me, too."

"I'll go talk to Josiah Bradley about his mares this—" She stopped abruptly, staring past his shoulder. She tossed the reins over the fence rail and in the same motion braced both hands on the top rung. She vaulted up and over in an instant and bolted across the adjoining pasture, leaving Jed to stare after her in astonishment.

"Kate!" Jessie cried anxiously, skidding to a stop by her side. The young woman appeared pale and shaken. "Are you all right?"

Kate gave a tremulous smile. "Yes," she said just a bit uncertainly. "I think so. Perhaps a little too much sun."

Jessie glanced at the clear sky and felt the skitter of a breeze across her cheek. "It's not that warm, Kate," she said with concern, her fingers brushing Kate's hand. Her blue eyes darkened with worry. "You're shaking."

Taking a deep breath, Kate smiled for real. "I'm fine. Truly." She felt foolish now, appearing fragile when it wasn't that at all. She tried not to think about the fact that Jessie's light touch on her hand had started the falling sensations all over again. She pointed towards the corral, wanting to change the subject. "What was that you were doing in there?"

Jessie followed her gaze to where Jed was pulling the saddle off the stallion she had been riding. "Just working him out under saddle. I'm planning on buying him and a few others with similar bloodlines. I wanted to see how he'd handle."

Kate was afraid that anything she said would sound inane, but she didn't think she had ever seen anything as beautiful as Jessie Forbes on that horse. "I want to take your picture," she blurted without thinking.

"What?" Jessie exclaimed. "Me?" She stared at Kate, astonished. Then she laughed. "Oh, Kate! Why on earth would you want to do that? With all this beautiful country around here, you want to take a picture of a dusty trail hand?"

"You're beautiful, too," Kate said quite seriously. When Jessie blushed, Kate hurried on. "You are...I mean...the way you look on that horse, like the two of you were born connected. It's...it's..." she stopped in frustration. *Why is it so hard to put words to the way I feel about you?*

"Kate," Jessie said quietly. "If it would please you to take my picture, then I won't say no."

Kate's brilliant smile was Jessie's reward. "This afternoon?"

"Whenever you want." Jessie laughed again. "Should I
change my clothes? I'll be riding all morning, and by then I'll be
a sight."

Remembering how Jessie had looked in a sweat-dampened
shirt, Kate shook her head. "No," she said softly, shyly now. "I
want you just like that."

⌘ ❖ ◆ ❖ ◆ ❖ ◆ ⌘

"Millie, could you let me have two of your sandwiches?"
Kate asked. "I'll take over here for you tomorrow morning in
return."

Millie was a new bride, the young wife of the town marshal.
She was rumored to make the best brisket in town, and her stand
was a popular one with the cowboys. She had been one of the
first women in town to befriend Kate, and being of a similar age,
they made easy companions.

"Of course, Kate." Millie regarded Kate with a knowing
smile. "Two, is it? You aren't trying to bribe your way into some
man's heart with one of those, are you?"

Kate colored self-consciously. "No, I'm taking one for
Jessie Forbes."

"Well," Millie announced, packing a basket, "if she's anything like my Tom after a day on a horse, you'd best take three."

"Thank you, Millie," Kate said, gathering the basket of
food.

"Of course, silly. Oh! Don't forget the dance tomorrow
night. Everyone will be there."

Kate smiled, her eyes fixed on the auction yard, her mind on
Jessie. "I won't forget."

It was the biggest auction day of the week, and the yard was
packed. Kate walked to the edge of the crowd surrounding the
auction platform. She watched as several prize steers, or so the
auctioneer claimed, were auctioned off at apparently high prices.
Kate found it hard to follow the bidding because men seemed to
signal without saying anything.

"Now, gentlemen," the auctioneer called, "the last sale of the afternoon, and the one you've been waiting for, I imagine. I'm offering the best brood mare this side of the Mississippi. She's gonna throw the finest foals this territory has ever seen. Do I hear an opening bid?"

Kate heard a murmur pass through the crowd, and she saw Jessie, across the yard, touch her hat brim nonchalantly. Jessie had one heel up on the railing and was leaning an arm over the top post, looking relaxed and casual. The bidding became rapid, and Kate lost track of the amount, but every now and then she saw Jessie touch her hat. Finally the bidding slowed, and the crowd quieted.

"Do I hear another bid, gentlemen?" the auctioneer called. "Any other bids? Going once, going twice, SOLD!" He looked Jessie's way and shouted, "To the Rising Star ranch!"

Jessie broke into a smile and turned to the cowboy beside her, who pumped her hand vigorously before walking off toward the holding pens. As the crowd started to disperse, Kate picked her way carefully across the yard. Jessie watched her approach, too happy to contain a wide grin.

"Hello, Kate."

Kate was always surprised at the deep, mellow quality of Jessie's voice. She tilted her head back to look up into Jessie's face and said a little breathlessly, "Is that the horse you wanted?"

"Yep, she is. I've been waiting almost two years to find the right animal, and this is the one."

"I'm glad for you," Kate said, meaning it. She lifted her napkin draped wicker basket. "I brought some sandwiches. If you're going to pose for me, I thought I should feed you first."

Jessie looked surprised and then pleased. "I could do with something to eat. I've been so worked up over the bidding today I think I forgot all about my stomach." She frowned. "Where's your camera and all?"

"I left it back at the tables. We can get it after we eat."

"I'm about ready for that right now."

Impulsively, Kate threaded her arm through Jessie's. "Good. Then let's find a nice quiet place to celebrate your new purchase."

For an instant, Jessie went utterly still. The nearness of Kate's body was completely strange to her. She never would have thought that the soft touch of a woman's hand could make her feel so tall.

"I think that's a fine idea, Kate," Jessie said softly.

Chapter
10

A short walk from town, they found a secluded spot under a cluster of trees at the very base of the foothills that climbed precipitously toward the towering mountain peaks. Jessie helped Kate spread out a cloth on the ground. Above them, the sky was a deep blue dotted here and there with dollops of white frothy clouds. There were no sounds save for the faint buzzing of insects and the far away lowing of the cattle in the pens.

"I'm glad that you suggested we bring the camera with us," Kate observed, unfolding the legs of the support. "Now that we're here, I don't want to go back for anything. It's a perfect spot, and I can't wait to get started."

Jessie watched the process, hands in the back pockets of her levis, a curious look on her face. "I still think my horses would make a prettier picture."

Kate merely smiled and gestured to a spot where she could see the mountaintop behind them. "Right over there, please." She positioned the camera, framing Jessie in the foreground. "No, leave your hat on. Just tip it back a bit." She looked up, meeting Jessie's gaze. "I like you in that hat."

The hint of teasing, and something else—something warm— in Kate's voice, caused Jessie to blush. "What should I do with my hands?" she asked to cover her embarrassment.

Kate lifted the cloth over her head and, in a muffled voice called, "Just stand like you were talking to Jed. Pretend I'm not here."

"That would be some kind of trick, for sure," Jessie muttered.

Kate laughed. "And don't talk."

Through the lens, Kate focused on Jessie. Isolated under the black covering, Kate was alone with her in a way that was so strangely intimate it made her pulse flutter. She was struck anew by Jessie's confident carriage and supple strength. The rancher was unlike anyone, man or woman, Kate had ever known. She was so beautiful it made Kate's throat ache.

With a trembling hand, she opened the shutter and counted softly to herself. For a few seconds after she finished the exposure, she continued to gaze at her, absorbing every detail of her face and body. Finally she called, "We're done." Her voice sounded strange to her own ears, and she was aware of unsettled warmth in her depths.

"Can't say as I mind," Jessie remarked, but her tone was light. She stretched out on the ground next to the makeshift tablecloth, enjoying the breeze that played over her face. She sighed, inexplicably content. "Seems like an age since I've stopped more than a minute in one spot."

Kate sat down beside her and placed the basket of food between them. She studied Jessie's face, catching the weary undertones in her voice. Jessie had tossed her hat behind her and was on her back, one arm behind her head, her long legs sprawled out in front of her. Her eyes were closed, her hair a thick golden mane that framed her tanned face, just touching her collar. A patch of pale skin on her upper chest that the sun hadn't touched was exposed where the shirt lay open. She looked terribly vulnerable, and Kate suddenly realized that for all Jessie's ability and strength, she was still but a woman barely older than herself. *And a very tired one.*

"Are you all right, Jessie?" she asked softly, her voice husky with concern.

Jessie turned her head toward Kate, her lids fluttering open. She found herself looking up into Kate's deep, dark eyes, and for a moment she did not answer. Kate's skin was the most beautiful color that Jessie had ever seen, rich as fresh cream. Her black hair and brows emphasized her loveliness, and Jessie thought of a picture of angels she had seen in one of her father's books. Just now, however, Kate's eyes were cloudy, and there was a little frown line above her nose. Jessie smiled then, a brilliant smile that chased the shadows from Kate's eyes.

"I'm fine, Kate. This has been a hard week for my ranch. I've sold or traded most of my stock, and there were a few deals I wasn't sure I could make. But I think it's over now."

"You'll be leaving soon, won't you?" Kate asked, her expression darkening even more.

Jessie leaned up on one elbow, nodding. "The day after tomorrow. The men have let off some steam, and we all have a lot of work to do when we get back."

"Of course." Kate looked away, her hands tightening in her lap. "I see."

Now Jessie was troubled. Seeing Kate upset bothered her more than she could say. "Kate, is something wrong?"

She turned to Jessie, her cheeks flushed. "Oh Jessie, don't pay any attention to me. It's just that all this will be over then." Her eyes were suddenly, inexplicably, swimming with tears. "And...and you'll be gone, too," she finished softly.

"Kate, I...I..." Jessie hesitantly touched the back of her hand to the single drop that had escaped Kate's long lashes, trailing unheeded down her cheek. "Kate," Jessie whispered, a tightness in her chest so heavy she thought she would stop breathing.

Kate placed her fingers gently on Jessie's. "Shh, never mind. It's not your fault."

Jessie's eyes widened at the touch of Kate's hand. The air grew thick, and a fine tremor began in her fingers. Her head buzzed like it did when she'd been too long in the saddle in the August heat.

Time stopped for Kate, every sound stilled, as she gazed at Jessie, frozen. She could see so clearly the quick rise and fall of her chest beneath the cotton shirt. She wanted desperately to run her fingers over the bruise that still lingered on Jessie's cheek, but she didn't dare move. If Jessie took her hand from Kate's skin, Kate feared she would die. As they leaned toward one another, their gazes locked. Kate knew her face was high with color, but all she could think about was Jessie's eyes. *How could anyone's eyes be so blue?*

Mesmerized, Jessie felt as if she were falling with nothing to hold onto. Her legs trembled so much she could not have stood. Something inside her stirred, hungry and scared all at once. Her blood ran hot and fierce with a want for which she had no name. She pulled away, struggling with an army of sensations she had never known.

Kate's hand fell back into her lap.

"The sandwiches..." Jessie mumbled, reaching toward the basket.

"Yes," Kate answered, her voice unsteady.

They finished their lunch and walked back into town, each of them quiet.

"You will come to the dance, won't you?" Kate asked finally as they prepared to part. They stood very close, but they did not touch. "Before you go?"

Jessie nodded. "I'll be there."

"Promise?" Kate asked with a smile that hid her anxiety. *Oh, how I don't want you to go.*

"I promise, Kate," Jessie said with an answering smile of her own.

Kate did touch her then, a light brush of her fingers along Jessie's arm. "Good," she said as she stepped away.

Jessie watched Kate leave, wondering why it seemed like something was tearing loose inside her. She stood there for a long time in the gathering dusk, feeling more alone than she could ever remember.

Chapter 11

"Martha! We'll be late if we don't leave soon!"

Martin and Kate were impatiently pacing the length of the sitting room, dressed and ready to go. Martin didn't want to miss a moment of the night's festivities. Kate hadn't been able to think of anything all day except that this was Jessie's last night in town and it would be so dreary after she and the other cowboys left.

"Well, Kate. Since almost everyone in town will be at the dance tonight, it will be like your coming out ball all over again." He smiled approvingly at his daughter. "You look lovely."

She wore a midnight-blue dress that her mother had carefully packed and carried all the way from Boston. It was elegant in its simplicity, cut away at the neck only enough to show a hint of bodice, the skirt skimming her slender form in the latest style. Kate had worn it once before but not with the anticipation she did now. Tonight, she felt like a woman and not like a young girl on display.

"I think after this evening we'll be seeing more than a few young men appearing at our door," Martin enthused, beaming with fatherly pride.

Kate smiled at him, dismissing the question of suitors with

an easy shrug. "We shall never know if we don't get there, Father. I'll go see what's keeping Mother."

She left Martin peering at his watch and made her way upstairs to her mother's room. Martha was seated before her dressing table, dressed to go.

"Mother, is something wrong? Are you ill?" Kate was frightened by the strange look on her mother's face.

Martha turned to Kate and smiled slightly. "Frightened I think, Kate. You and your father have settled in so well; it's as if you've always lived here. We've been here for weeks, and I still feel like a stranger. Oh, everyone is kind and helpful, but I feel out of place. Tonight, with the whole town there, I'm not sure I can manage." She shook her head helplessly.

Kate crossed the room quietly and put gentle hands on her mother's shoulders. "You expect too much of yourself, Mother. There's no hurry. You'll discover in time that these people are really no different than those we knew in Boston. You have to look past their clothes and their different ways and see them for the honest, good people that they are." She met her mother's eyes in the mirror. "I don't expect you'll like all of them, but I think you'll find most of them can be friends. Some of them are quite extraordinary." She gave her mother a comforting pat, laughing. "Come on now, before Father explodes."

Martha followed her daughter downstairs, far from convinced, but determined to make the best of her situation. It was clear to her that her husband and her daughter had already made New Hope their home.

⌘ ❖ ♦ ❖ ♦ ❖ ♦ ⌘

Jessie packed her valise and stood it at the foot of the bed. She planned to leave in the morning and had already settled her accounts at the bank. She'd only stayed tonight because of the town gathering and dance. It was a town tradition to celebrate the end of roundup, and despite the fact that she didn't know most of the townspeople any more than to say hello, she had been raised to respect tradition. And she had promised Kate that she would be there.

Thinking of Kate made her smile. There was something so fresh and eager about Kate that when they were together everything seemed so much more exciting than it ever had before. No one had ever made her feel at once so comfortable and so alive. She knew there were other feelings Kate stirred in her, but, not knowing how to explain them, she set them aside. Soon, she would be back at the ranch, and she would probably never see Kate again, except to nod hello in the street when they might happen to meet. Unaccountably saddened by the realization, she turned to the mirror above the dresser and surveyed her reflection, determined not to think about anything except the evening ahead.

She wore a black shirt with silver trim at the pockets and cuffs, tucked into close-fitting black pants. Her blond hair was tied loosely at the back of her neck with a black ribbon. The heavy beaten silver trim on her ornate holster matched the shimmering silver threads in her shirt. *I look like a tenderfoot,* she thought ruefully, but she was not displeased. She reached for her black hat, walked out, and closed her door.

When she arrived at the meetinghouse, she found the crowd was already spilling out into the street. Music and the muted roar of many voices wafted out through the open double doors. She sidled her way through the crowd, nodding and exchanging hellos with wranglers she knew and townspeople she recognized. After entering the large crowded room, she made her way slowly around the periphery. In the center of the space, people jostled and talked and surrounded those couples dancing to the lively music of several fiddlers.

Nearing the tables in the rear where women offered food and drink, she suddenly realized that she was very hungry. A robust arm reached out for her, and she turned, meeting twinkling blue eyes and a broad smile.

"Jessie Forbes! You look mighty fine tonight," Hannah Schroeder bellowed above the roar. "I heard that you did well at the auction this year. I'm pleased to hear it!"

Jessie broke into a smile and shouted back, "Thank you, and your husband, too. I would say I'm pleased enough with how the Rising Star did!"

Hannah nodded again and piled food on a plate. As she handed it to Jessie, she seemed to remember something and shouted again, "Jessie, I forgot to introduce you two. This here is Mrs. Martin Beecher. She and her family are new in town. Martha, this is Jessie Forbes, one of the ranchers from north of here."

Jessie looked quickly at Martha, who was staring at her intently, and doffed her hat. Now she could see the resemblance to Kate in that dark hair and penetrating gaze. "Ma'am," she said politely. "I'm pleased to know you. I hope you're settling in well."

Martha struggled to absorb the idea of a woman striding about in public dressed like a man, and carrying a weapon. *Different, Kate had said? Indecent was more like it. Lord, what were people thinking of out here.*

"How do you do, Miss Forbes," she answered stiffly. She turned away gratefully when a new arrival extended a plate for her to fill. All she could think was how relieved she would be when all this roundup business was over and these cowboys would leave town.

Unabashed, Jessie stared after her for a second. She then nodded to Hannah and moved off to a quiet corner of the room to eat.

Kate had been watching for Jessie to arrive all evening, and when she first saw her, she caught her breath sharply in surprise. She had not known what to expect, but certainly not this. Jessie appeared neither as a dusty trail hand nor as another frontier woman in her best Sunday dress. Jessie was just herself—striking in shimmering black and silver, confident and sure. She stood slightly apart from the crowd and, in Kate's eyes, was the most interesting person in the room. Kate stepped quietly away from the group of young women she was with and made her way through the crowd toward her.

Jessie leaned back against a broad wooden pole, a little away from the edge of the dance floor, listening to the music and trying to relax. A cool evening breeze drifted in from an open window nearby. She looked over the crowd, searching for Kate. She hadn't thought about much else all day except that she would see Kate that night, and she couldn't stop worrying over their strange lunch the day before. Something was troubling Kate, and that troubled *her* more than anything ever had.

At that moment, Jessie spied her approach and forgot completely what she had been fretting about. Kate was a vision in blue, easily the loveliest woman in the room, and the smile she sent Jessie's way set her heart to pounding strangely.

"I thought you might not come," Kate said breathlessly, her eyes searching Jessie's face.

"And what else would I do during the biggest gathering of the year?" Jessie asked teasingly. She grinned a little shyly. "Besides, I told you that I would be here."

"Yes, you did," Kate said softly. She knew absolutely that this woman would always keep her word.

Jessie looked down at her, surprised by the wistful note in her voice. "Is something wrong?"

"No," Kate answered with a quick shake of her head, determined to enjoy their time together. She'd been thinking of nothing else for days. "Everything is fine."

"Good," Jessie said, smiling. "I'm so glad to see you."

"You look beautiful tonight. I like you in black." Kate said it quietly, realizing she really meant it. *Odd,* she thought, *ordinarily I don't notice such things. Jessie has a way of capturing my attention without doing anything more than smiling at me.*

Blushing under her tan, Jessie looked away. She wasn't used to the kind of admiring glance Kate was giving her. It seemed as if she could feel Kate's eyes moving over her body, and it was doing funny things to her breathing. When she spoke, her voice was thick and low.

"I'd say *beautiful* was more what you are tonight, Kate." Her heart raced as her gaze traveled from Kate's eyes, dark and deep with feeling, to her full lips, curled into a faint smile. Dimly, she was aware of blood pounding in her ears as she watched the hypnotic rise and fall of Kate's breasts against the brilliant blue of the dress. "You glow."

Kate couldn't look away from her. The sound of Jessie's voice was all that she could hear, the blue of Jessie's eyes all that she could see. She took a step closer. Her head was even with Jessie's shoulder; she watched the pulse beat quickly in Jessie's neck.

Jessie's right hand was curled tightly around her silver studded belt, so tightly her fingers ached. She drew breath in sharply as she felt Kate's fingers, feather light on her own, but she didn't move.

Kate's eyes were sparkling black diamonds, and her face was misted with a fine perspiration. She reached her other hand slowly, intent on touching the pulse fluttering hypnotically in Jessie's throat. Her hand was inches from Jessie's skin, fingers trembling faintly. "Jessie—"

"Why, Miss Beecher..." a male voice interjected.

Kate's hand stilled and Jessie jerked her head around.

"You look too pretty tonight to be standing off here all alone. I think you should be dancing. May I have that pleasure?" Ken Turner, the town's only lawyer and himself a relative newcomer, was smiling confidently at Kate, waiting expectantly.

"I'm not alone," Kate retorted hotly, not bothering to hide her anger at his rude intrusion. "I'm talking with—"

"He's quite right, Kate." Jessie quickly pulled her hand from under Kate's, took a step back, and added quietly, "This is a party, and you *should* be dancing. Please go ahead."

Kate glanced at Jessie, unable to decipher the remote expression in her eyes. She didn't know how to politely refuse Ken Turner's request, although leaving Jessie to dance with him was the last thing she wanted to do. Nodding a silent assent to the man beside her, she took his arm, letting him lead her to the dance floor. As she followed, she struggled with her anger and confusion. She had not wanted to dance with him, and she did not understand why Jessie suggested that she should. Feigning civility as he placed his arm lightly around her waist, Kate looked back to where Jessie had been standing. She was gone.

⌘ ❖ ♦ ❖ ♦ ❖ ♦ ⌘

Jessie pushed through the swinging doors of the saloon and surveyed the empty room. Even Frank the bartender was at the dance. She walked behind the bar and poured a brandy, leaving a coin on the polished top. She pulled out a chair, sat at one of the tables, and stared into the dark amber liquid swirling in her glass. She wasn't sure how long she'd been there when she heard footsteps on the stairs behind her.

"Well, Montana," Mae softly called as she made her way behind the bar. She pulled a bottle down from the shelf. "You're home early from the dance."

"I didn't much feel like it tonight, Mae."

"Oh? And everyone's there, too." Mae tried to read the thoughts behind Jessie's impassive features and failed. She poured herself a whiskey and came around to sit down on Jessie's right.

"Something happen tonight, Jess?" she asked casually, noting the hollow tone in Jessie's voice. She sipped the whiskey and watched her friend's face, knowing Jessie was too honest to hide much.

"What?" Jessie asked, as if from far away. She couldn't find the words to describe how she felt, even to herself. Empty, in a funny sort of way. "Oh, no. Just tired, I guess."

"Maybe you've had too much of this easy town living. Maybe you're just homesick for a rocky bed and cold food," Mae teased lightly.

Jessie looked fondly at Mae. "Maybe that's it, Mae. Too much comfort can be bad for you." She stretched her legs out under the table and shrugged her tense shoulders. "Maybe I do just need to get back to the ranch where I belong."

Mae got up and stood behind the lanky rancher, her hands resting lightly on tight shoulders. She gently kneaded the stiff muscles, leaning close to murmur, "Tell you what *I* think you need. A good old-fashioned bath. Finish your drink now. One of the girls was just drawing me a hot tub upstairs. The way these muscles are strung, you feel like you could use it more than me."

Eyes closed, Jessie sighed softly and leaned back. Mae's hands felt good, and she *was* weary. "You'll have me asleep here in a minute, Mae."

Mae stared down at Jessie's finely chiseled features and stroked her fingers lightly over the silky smooth skin of her neck. Minutes passed and Jessie remained motionless, her slender hands resting quietly on her thighs, her head resting gently against Mae's body. Finally moving her hand, she whispered with effort, "Come on, Montana. I'll give you a hand with that bath."

Jessie shuddered and roused herself. She followed Mae slowly up the stairs, but her mind was still on the dance and the way that Kate had looked in Ken Turner's arms. She had no idea why it bothered her so much that she wouldn't get to say good-bye.

"Shed those duds," Mae instructed as she tested the temperature of the water, then added a little more from a still-steaming kettle set on the fireplace hearth in the far corner of the room. "And climb in here."

The weary rancher stripped, laying her clothes over the chair next to the bed. She lowered herself into the tin tub, sighing. "That does feel good."

Mae stood behind her, working up a lather with a bar of soap. "Dunk your head."

Jessie did, then shook the water from her eyes and rested her neck on the rim, stretching her arms out along the sides. The water came to just above her breasts. She closed her eyes as Mae washed her hair, groaning softly in appreciation. She drifted with the heat and the soothing rhythm of Mae's fingers on her scalp.

Watching as Jessie's limbs loosened and her breathing became slow and deep, Mae gently rinsed the soap from thick sun-streaked hair, smoothing the stray strands off Jessie's face. She rested her palms very lightly on Jessie's shoulders, her fingers trailing over the edge of collar bone, just brushing the pale skin of her upper chest. Jessie shifted, sighing faintly. Mae held her breath for a long moment, her hands trembling, then murmured, "Jessie."

Jessie heard the soft voice call to her from a long ways away. She smiled up into the face so close to hers, responding to the welcoming gaze with a swift rush of pleasure. She lifted her hand and caught the fingers that stroked her skin, turning the palm and pressing it to her lips. She was warm, warm and liquid deep within, and her limbs trembled with a sweet urgency that grew more insistent as she drew the hand she held onto her breast. She tilted her head, eager for a kiss from the lips so near her own. With the first gentle pressure on her mouth, she sighed again, the breath stealing from her body on the wings of desire.

"Wake up, Montana," Mae repeated, louder this time.

Jessie came awake with a start, sitting up so suddenly that water splashed over the rim onto the floor. "Lord," she muttered, looking wildly about. Mae stood beside her, a towel in her hand. "What happened?"

"You fell asleep," Mae said matter-of-factly.

"That's all?" Jessie asked, trying to piece together the fragments of the dream. All she could clearly recall were wisps of color—blue skies, white bits of clouds, and dark eyes that held her. Eyes that were very different from Mae's deep green ones. Her body was quivering strangely, and she thought her skin might catch fire from the inside. She drew a ragged breath, reached for the towel, and stepped from the tub on trembling legs. "You sure?"

"What else?" Mae inquired, heading for the door. She wasn't about to tell Jessie whose name she had murmured in her sleep. There wasn't any point to giving her ideas if she didn't already have them. The one way Jessie differed from the cowboys she rode with was that she was sweetly unschooled in matters of the flesh. Mae loved Jessie's innocence as much as it sometimes tried her. "You were just dreaming, Jess."

Jessie stared at the door as it closed behind her friend, the memory of a kiss still tingling on her lips.

Chapter
12

"Kate, Kate darling! You must go upstairs and get ready. Mr. Turner will be here for dinner any moment, and you don't want him finding you like that," Martha called. She frowned as Kate turned away from the window where she had been sitting most of the afternoon, silent and withdrawn.

As her daughter disappeared obediently upstairs, Martha turned to Martin, who sat before the fireplace, engrossed in the paper. "Martin, I'm worried about Kate. She has been so quiet these last few weeks. She spends most of her time in that dark room with her pictures, and she rarely visits any of her new friends. I do believe she's losing weight. She needs to get out more."

Martin glanced up and chuckled. "Haven't you noticed all this mooning about started shortly after the dance last month? Just about the time young Ken Turner started calling? I should think you'd recognize the way a young girl acts when she's being courted." He smiled and shook his head. "And I must say, I like that Turner. He's got a fine head on his shoulders and a promising future in this town. He'd make a very good husband for Kate."

Looking exasperated, Martha wasn't as convinced as her husband about the cause of Kate's moodiness. She indeed knew how young girls in love acted. They might moon about, but only when it suited them. She saw none of the excitement in Kate's eyes that should have been there when Ken Turner came to call and none of the eagerness for his visits that was expected. The lawyer gave every indication that his intent was serious where Kate was concerned. Kate, for her part, was polite and attentive, as was proper and expected under the circumstances, but when alone, she was melancholic.

"I'm not so sure, Martin. Kate isn't acting at all like herself." Martha hoped that Kate hadn't gotten some romantic notion about love confused with practicality. Marriage was the first priority. Fondness would follow, as it had for her and Martin.

Martin sighed, went to his wife, and put his arms around her. "Don't worry, my dear. No reason in the world why she shouldn't take to Ken Turner, and given time, she'll see that, too."

⌘ ❖ ♦ ❖ ♦ ❖ ♦ ⌘

"I'm sorry," Kate said, blushing. "What did you say?"

Sitting with her parents and Ken Turner in the parlor after dinner, Kate found her mind wandering. She was restless and had a hard time paying attention to the usual topics of conversation that invariably included discussions of the weather, the newspaper business, and the increasing lawlessness along the Overland Trail. As the conversation went on around her, she wondered why she wasn't feeling what she should for Ken Turner. He was pleasant and amusing, and her parents approved of him. He had all the attributes of a proper suitor.

However, when he looked at her with fond regard, she felt like a bird in a trap. She wanted to flee, from his appraising glances and her parents' expectant expressions, and realized with ever deepening dread that she had nowhere to go. She tried to imagine being married to him, for surely that was why he continued to call, and she couldn't. She could not imagine waking up next to him in the morning or talking with him over breakfast, and she could not, no matter how hard she tried, imagine lying with him in the night. When he kissed her cheek before leaving in the evening, she had to force herself not to recoil from his touch.

"I'm sorry?" she repeated.

"Mr. Turner was asking about the help you've been giving Millie down at the school," Martha chided gently.

"Oh, yes," Kate replied, trying to sound enthusiastic. In truth, helping Millie Roberts was the only thing preserving her sanity, or so it seemed to her. "There are so many more children now, and since she's expecting her own soon, Millie needed help. I've been teaching reading, and I love it."

"Admirable," Ken remarked heartily. "A very fine thing for you to do until a regular teacher can be found, and you yourself are married."

Kate stared at him, at a loss as to how to respond. It was true that teaching was usually considered an occupation for unmarried women, since women rarely held any kind of employment after marriage. Millie, she knew, had only stayed on because the town hadn't been able to find a replacement. She had never understood why marriage meant a woman could not work outside the home, and as she considered her own future, it made even less sense. She could not see herself living her mother's life or even the lives of her friends like Millie. *What is wrong with me?*

She looked at the handsome young man in her parents' parlor and thought about the evening they had met. The only thing she could recall about the entire evening was a tall, blond woman in black and silver. *Jessie.* Kate hadn't even had the chance to say goodbye.

The morning after the dance, she had hurried to the hotel, asking for Jessie, only to be told the rancher was gone. She had rushed through town to the auction yards, desolate when she found that the pens were all empty. With a sinking feeling, she had surveyed the gates standing open and the deserted corrals. Right then, a sadness had settled upon her that would not lift. She ached, and longed for something she could not name.

She had not seen Jessie since, but her memory of her was as clear as one of her photos. She kept looking for her every time a cowboy rode into town or she heard the jingle of spurs on the sidewalk behind her. When she lay down to sleep, she remembered the glow in Jessie's eyes as they stood close together, their hands lightly touching. She would find that she was shivering, first hot, then cold, her heart racing. Her dreams were filled with strange half-visions of long, slender fingers, golden hair and blue, blue eyes. She would awaken in the morning even more unsettled, with a curious trembling in her stomach. *What is happening?*

"Kate, Kate!" Martha looked at her daughter with concern. "Mr. Turner has asked to see some of your photos, dear."

Kate forced a bright smile. "Of course. How kind. I'll bring some out for you." She escaped gratefully for a few moments to her room, counting the minutes until she could be alone again.

⌘ ❖ ◆ ❖ ◆ ❖ ◆ ⌘

Jessie paced uneasily back and forth on the broad porch that fronted her home. It was late, and the night was still under a black sky broken only by the faraway flicker of summer stars. For some reason, she couldn't read; her mind kept losing the thread. Her insides were churning, and even a bit of whiskey couldn't settle her. She had taken to riding hours on the open range every day, checking fences that didn't need mending and riding herd on horses that didn't need tending. She slept poorly and was short-tempered, flaring up at Jed over nothing at all. Even the sight of the sun setting over the land she loved failed to calm her. This land, her home, which had always been her comfort, seemed empty and barren.

The sound of her boots on the wood floors echoed aimlessly off the walls, and she was lonely. She sighed deeply and looked about her. She was tired, but she knew she wouldn't sleep. Instead, she walked to the barn and saddled her horse. She'd ride more, and maybe she'd no longer feel the ache.

Hours later, she dismounted in front of the saloon in New Hope. It was near to closing, and the bar was almost empty when she entered. She smiled wanly at Frank's surprised face as she leaned against the bar. "Evening, Frank. Got any of that brandy left?"

"Sure thing, Jessie. Kind of surprised to see you in here tonight."

"Me, too. I just started out from the ranch, and this is where I ended up."

He didn't comment. He'd been a bartender long enough to know that sometimes a cowboy just got tired of the silence out there in the night. He poured her a drink and filled her in on some of the local news.

Jessie listened and nodded, letting the warm glow of the brandy take the worry from her mind.

"Buy a lady a drink, Montana?"

Jessie smiled, her spirits lifting. She turned to Mae, nodding. "I sure will, if you'll sit and drink it with me, Mae."

Mae's sharp glance took in the circles under Jessie's eyes and the uneasy expression even the liquor couldn't smooth away. "You know there's nothing I'd like better, Jess. What brings you in here this time of week? Ranching getting too quiet for you?"

"Couldn't sleep," she admitted. "Didn't know what I wanted 'til I ended up here."

"Oh?" Mae's eyebrows arched as she said in a slightly mocking tone, "And what might that be?"

Jessie flushed, suddenly shy. "A friendly voice and a warm smile, I think."

Mae took Jessie's arm in hers and led her to a corner table. She lifted her glass to her lips and stared intently into Jessie's troubled eyes. "I'd say you've got something on your mind. Want to talk about it?"

"I don't know, Mae. I haven't been right lately. You know I love the ranch, and the work has always made me happy. These last few weeks I've felt sort of uneasy, like something was missing. Can't seem to get my head clear." Jessie looked down at the table, confused.

"Maybe you're just expecting too much from it. Work can't be everything to a person. I'd say you need a little relaxing now and then. Never could figure how a body could work as hard as you do."

Jessie laughed and tipped her brandy glass. Suddenly, she

didn't feel quite so alone. She bought them both another drink, and they sat and talked and waited for the sun to come up.

Finally, Jessie arched her back and looked out toward the street. "Lord, Mae. I've kept you up the whole night."

A small smile played across Mae's face. She swallowed the last of her drink and answered slowly, "Can't think of anyone else I'd rather spend the night with, Jess."

Jessie looked into her green eyes and felt herself grinning like a fool. "I'll remember that, Mae."

As she walked Jessie to the door and watched her walk out into the morning, Mae answered softly, "You be sure and do that, Montana."

Chapter 13

Martin groaned softly and turned over, struggling to ignore the pounding in his head. At last, he gave in and opened one eye. It was then that he realized that the barrage was coming from his front porch. He reached for his watch on the nightstand and was astounded to see that it was not yet six in the morning.

"Who could that be?" Martha queried anxiously from beside him as she sat up, the coverlet clutched protectively to her chest.

"I'll go see," he muttered, searching on the floor for his slippers.

Kate's bedroom door opened, and she peeked out, bleary-eyed and confused. "What is it?"

Martin shook his head, trudging sleepily to the stairs. "Don't know, my dear."

Kate pulled her robe tightly closed over her nightgown and followed her father down the stairs. Through the curtains covering the window in the front door, she recognized Thaddeus Schroeder's large form. He was raising his fist to bang again on the frame, simultaneously rattling the doorknob. The entire door shook on its hinges.

"Wait a minute!" Martin bellowed as he fit the key to the lock.

"Martin!" Thaddeus shouted before the door was half open.

"Get dressed. We've got to put out a special edition of the paper. There's news, man."

"What's happened?" Martin asked, instantly awake and turning back toward the stairs. "Let me get into some clothes."

Thaddeus followed into the foyer, calling after him, "A stagecoach was held up not far outside of town. It was on its way from the territorial seat in Bannack with some fellows from the land title office. They were carrying a fair amount of cash."

"The stage," Martin exclaimed, turning back at the top of the stairs. "But who?"

Thaddeus shook his head angrily. "Outlaws from further west in the territory. Men who couldn't find gold on their own and decided to steal it. They held up the coach and scared the passengers half to death. Robbed them and then were fixing to shoot them all. Imagine that." He glanced impatiently at his friend. "Come on, Martin, we've got to get down to Doc's office."

Martin frowned. "Doctor Melbourne? What for?"

Thaddeus gave him an impatient look. "Because a couple of folks got shot up. I told you those boys were looking for trouble."

Martin's face went pale. This was a little more excitement than he had been prepared for. "Shot? My Lord, Thaddeus, who?"

Thaddeus looked even more distressed. "The driver—Bill Marley—and Jessie Forbes."

Kate felt the blood drain from her face, and she sat down quickly on the stairs, her head buzzing. She was dimly aware of her father rushing down the hall toward his bedroom, of her mother's frightened voice calling questions, of Thaddeus shouting something in the background about Jessie. She pulled herself up using the banister and waited for her head to stop swirling.

"Mr. Schroeder," she gasped, her voice shaking, "Mr. Schroeder..."

"Yes, Kate?" Thaddeus responded distractedly, pacing at the foot of the stairs.

"Jessie. How is Jessie?" Kate held tightly to the railing, fearing that she might scream.

Thaddeus looked uncomfortable. "I don't know, Kate. She rode into it, apparently, and tried to stop the holdup. The marshal and some other men rode out with a wagon not long ago to get her and Marley. They should be coming into town soon." He stopped as Martin brushed past Kate and clambered down the stairs. Both men rushed out, slamming the door behind them.

She slumped against the wall, willing herself to think. In her mind's eye she saw Jessie—her blue eyes, her golden hair, her shy grin. Kate was not a stranger to death. In the arduous months of their journey west, she had seen accidents and illness claim the lives of men, women, and children. *But like this? Could the life of someone as gentle and kind as Jessie simply be snuffed out by men with no regard for law or morality?* For the first time, Kate understood that the bright new world she had discovered held evil, too, a darkness where death came quickly, without concern for goodness or justice.

"Oh, Lord," Kate whispered, afraid for the first time since leaving Boston. "Not Jessie. Please."

Her fear was what finally galvanized her. She rushed to her room and hastily pulled off her nightclothes. As she searched in her dresser for undergarments, she uncovered the photograph of Jessie she had taken the day of the picnic and then tucked away for safekeeping.

"Oh!" she gasped, lifting it tenderly in both hands. She stared at the image, her eyes slowly filling with tears as she recalled Jessie's easy smile and the soft touch of her hand as they sat side by side under a cloudless sky that had held no hint of tragedy. The memory was so powerful she trembled.

"Kate!" Martha called from the doorway of her daughter's room. "Where are you going at this hour?"

Kate crushed the photograph to her breast protectively and said without turning, "There's been a holdup. I'm going into town to see what's happening."

"That's no place for you," Martha admonished, more concerned for Kate's safety than propriety. "There may be trouble."

Kate finally faced her. "I must do something," she said stubbornly. "I can't stay here not knowing."

⌘ ❖ ◆ ❖ ◆ ❖ ◆ ⌘

A large crowd had gathered in the street, shifting and pulsating with a life of its own. Men stood on the steps in front of the marshal's office, waving rifles and shouting to others to form a posse. Men, women, and children milled about in front of the doctor's storefront office, craning for a view and talking excitedly all at once. Kate stood at the outskirts of the group, struggling to see, straining to hear any word of Jessie. With each second, her anxiety grew.

"Excuse me," she asked of a man nearby, "is there any news?"

He shook his head. "None for sure. Somebody's dead, but ain't no one saying who." He turned away as a swell of voices signaled that something was about to happen.

Kate's head was pounding so painfully she was afraid she would faint. Then she heard the rattle of wooden wheels on the rutted road and knew that the wagon was coming. She pushed her way through the crowd without thought for good manners or behavior. *I must see for myself or go mad!*

As she drew closer, she saw men lifting blanket-shrouded bodies out of the wagon bed and carrying them into one of the buildings. Her mind refused to register the horror of that image. She struggled her way to the side of the wagon and looked in, her eyes growing wide with fear as her breath caught painfully in her chest.

Jessie lay unconscious on the rough wooden boards, blood matted in her hair, a long gash just below her hairline, and an ugly dark hole in her shirt at the base of her left shoulder. Her chest and part of the blanket were soaked red. Her lips were white, and she was so still. So very still.

"Jessie," Kate whispered, an eternity of agony in her voice. "Oh no, Jessie."

Strangers reached in to gently lift Jessie from the wagon, and Kate heard her moan faintly. Kate bit her lip to stop a cry, her heart twisting at hearing Jessie's pain.

"Let me get a look at her," an irritated voice commanded as a harried looking middle-aged man shoved his way through the press of people. Kate recognized Doctor Melbourne. He looked under Jessie's shirt, shook his head worriedly, then looked up into the faces of the townspeople gathered around.

"I need one of you women to help me with her. She's got a bullet in her chest, and if we don't get it out, she's going to die. I can't have somebody fainting when I start digging, so make sure you can take it."

A blond woman with striking green eyes moved forward to the doctor's side and looked quickly at Jessie's inert form. She met his gaze squarely. "Let's get going then, Doc," she said calmly. "She's strong, but she ain't made of iron."

The doctor nodded, his face determined. "C'mon, Mae. We've got some work to do."

As they disappeared inside with Jessie, Kate stood staring after them. In the midst of the crowd, she felt helpless and terribly alone.

Chapter 14

Kate sat motionless on the same bench where she had been sitting a little more than two months ago when she had first seen Jessie Forbes. A lifetime ago, it seemed to her now. As she watched the door to the doctor's office, hoping for some word, she realized that all she had wanted these last few weeks had been to see Jessie again. As soon as Jessie had ridden out of town after the roundup, Kate missed her. Every day, as she went about her business—learning about her new home and her new responsibilities, helping Millie at the school, taking the occasional family portrait for new friends and neighbors, even entertaining Ken Turner—she missed her.

She missed her easy smile and her gentle way of talking and the way that she made Kate feel special. She missed looking at her in her dusty levis and work-dampened shirt and feeling her own heart race for no apparent reason. She missed the way the sound of Jessie's spurs jingling could make her stomach quiver in that oddly nice way. She missed the light touch of Jessie's fingers when they brushed over her hand and the warmth it started inside. She missed all of her.

Kate's mind was blank for long periods, and then suddenly, she would remember why she was waiting. Jessie was hurt. Her throat tightened and tears threatened to spill. Hours passed, but she had no real sense of the passage of time. The sun grew bright and hung high in the sky, casting a harsh, merciless light over the brown earth of the street. People passed by, some spoke to her, and she nodded automatically. Her eyes remained fixed on the door across the street.

Sometime in the morning, a group of men came galloping hard into town and clustered in a roiling pack in the street in front of the doctor's office. A man Kate had seen with Jessie at the roundup bolted inside while the others paced about outside. He came out a short time later and murmured something to the agitated men crowded around. Now, they were sitting on the stairs or leaning against the railings, smoking and waiting, too.

Kate struggled for a way to describe emotions for which she had no words. *What will I feel, if I never see Jessie again?* Without fully understanding it, she knew there would be an emptiness inside of her that would never be filled. She felt connected to Jessie in some deep way that she had never before experienced. *This can't happen,* she thought over and over. *Not now. Not when I'm just beginning to see.*

Trying to imagine the unimaginable, she had drifted so far into that unbearable place of loss that it took her several seconds to realize that the door across the street had opened. The blond woman, who had volunteered to help the doctor with Jessie, was talking to the waiting men gathered outside. Kate gave a small cry and jumped to her feet. *That woman would know about Jessie!*

As the woman started slowly down the street, Kate hurried after her, the hem of her dress lifted in both hands, higher than was proper, so that it would not trip her. She couldn't be bothered about how she looked now.

As Kate drew near, the woman's exhaustion became apparent. Her golden hair had fallen from its pins, tumbling in disarray over her bare shoulders. Her emerald green dress, far too revealing for walking about in, was rumpled and stained. Kate registered, in a distracted way, that she was quite beautiful.

Kate reached a trembling hand and touched the woman's arm. "Excuse me. I'm sorry," she said, her voice wavering. "Can you tell me how Jessie is?"

Mae turned, her eyes bleak. "She's alive, barely."

Kate swayed, suddenly dizzy. "Oh, thank God."

"God had nothing to do with it," Mae answered bitterly.

"Please," Kate persisted, fighting to clear her vision, "could you tell me..." Her voice trailed off as spots danced in front of her eyes. The turmoil of the day and the absence of any nourishment were making her light-headed.

Mae grasped the pale young woman's arm with a strong hand and peered at her closely, trying to remember where she had seen her before and wondering why she should be so upset. Mae sighed, too tired to be surprised by anything at the moment. "Right now, I need a drink, and from the looks of you, you could use one, too. Come with me."

Kate allowed herself to be led down the street, scarcely noticing their destination. Relief washed through her, and all she could see was Jessie's face. Mae took her down an alley and through a side door into the saloon. When she pointed to a table in the rear of the deserted room, Kate sank down gratefully.

Trudging to the bar, Mae slumped onto a stool. She pushed her hair away from her face wearily. "Frank, give me a tall whiskey. And a brandy."

Frank poured the drinks and looked at Mae cautiously. "You want me to get you something to eat, Mae? You look pretty done in."

The weary blond started to shake her head no and then caught sight of Kate's trembling figure. The girl looked like she might swoon any second. "Maybe a couple of sandwiches."

He nodded, then asked quietly, "Jessie gonna make it?"

She looked at him, a lifetime of sorrow written in her expression. "If there is any justice in this world, she will."

She took the drinks from him, crossed to where Kate was sitting, and put the brandy into Kate's hands. "Drink this."

Kate looked at it uncomprehendingly, still not herself.

"Come on, now," Mae said, not unkindly. "Drink it. Then we'll talk." She took a stiff gulp of her own drink and welcomed the fiery trail it burned down her throat. The pain was much better than the hopelessness she had felt looking at Jessie lying naked, a great gaping tear in her, while her blood ran red onto

Mae's hands. She closed her eyes and held the glass tightly, her fingers white.

Kate took a swallow. Her eyes widened and she coughed, half choking. Color flooded her face and she seemed to waken, as if from a dream. "Oh!" she exclaimed.

Mae opened her eyes and touched Kate's hand reassuringly. "First time's the hardest. Drink some more."

Kate gasped and took another sip. She straightened up a little and looked intently at Mae. Her mind was clear, although her stomach felt odd. "Would you tell me now, please?"

Smiling at Kate slightly, Mae heard the steel in her voice and thought that maybe she was tougher than she first appeared. Mae had a feeling she might like this young woman under other circumstances.

"Well," Mae said slowly, "Doc says the head injury was just a flesh wound and won't hurt her any in the long run. Her shoulder's pretty torn up, but he got the bullet out. It didn't do damage to any, uh, vital organs." She shook her head, trying to dispel the image of him probing in Jessie's shoulder with cold metal instruments while she held Jessie down. *How could a person live after something like that was done to her?* She was only thankful that Jess didn't seem to have had any awareness of it, only moaning softly as the doc worked.

"And she'll be all right?" Kate persisted, her eyes fixed on Mae's face, looking for the truth.

Mae sighed and finished her drink at a swallow. "The big problem, he said, was all that blood she lost. If she does all right through the night, she should get well."

"Then it's not over yet," Kate whispered softly, feeling something inside her grow hard and cold. "She'll be all right. I know she will."

Mae looked at the set to Kate's jaw and the way her spine stiffened. *The girl's got spirit, all right.* She walked to the bar and returned with a bottle, setting it down between them.

"Let's have another drink, sweetie."

Kate looked at her and smiled grimly. She held out her hand and said, "My name is Kate Beecher, by the way."

"Figured it might be," Mae said dryly and took her hand.

⌘ ❖ ♦ ❖ ♦ ❖ ♦ ⌘

Kate looked up as a man approached, his face set and grim. She recognized him from the doctor's office earlier that morning. He sat down across from Mae and nodded a weary greeting.

"I want to thank you, Mae. For what you did for Jess." His voice was very soft for such a big man.

"No need to thank me, Jed. Not when it's Jess," Mae said quietly. She turned to Kate. "This here is Jed Harper, Jessie's foreman. Jed, Miss Kate Beecher."

"Hello, Mr. Harper."

"Ma'am," he said absently, still looking fixedly at Mae. He continued angrily, "The damn doctor won't let me in there, Mae, and he won't say no more than that she's alive. What's going on?"

"I don't know much more than you do, Jed. We're just waitin', too." Her expression hardened. "Did they catch those bastards yet?"

Kate was shocked, at first, at the undisguised hatred in Mae's voice and then realized that she felt the same way. She looked at Jed expectantly.

"Ain't but one to catch, Mae," Jed said, laughing darkly. "Jess got one herself, with both of them firing on her, too. And from the looks of things, she got a piece of the other fella before...before he got her." His voice trembled and he looked away. He swallowed several times, then added, "I sure don't want nothin' to happen to that girl, Mae. I promised Tom I'd look after her, and...and...I think it's her been lookin' after me."

Mae put her hand on his shoulder and smiled a little. "You know how hard-headed Jess can be, Jed. I don't imagine she's going to leave things at the ranch up to you for long."

Jed's grateful glance bespoke his thanks. He took a deep breath, suddenly looking determined. "You know, I'd best get back out there and see to things, or she'll be madder'n a hornet when she gets home."

"I'd keep an eye on your men, too, Jed," Mae suggested sagely. "Jess wouldn't want them doing anything crazy if they catch this fella."

"No need to worry about the boys," he growled, his eyes hard. "When we get him, I'll take care of him myself."

Mae regarded him solemnly, then nodded. "Be careful."

"Thanks, Mae."

Kate watched him go. "Would he? Kill the man?"

"Probably," Mae said, studying Kate closely.

Kate was silent for a long moment. Then she said with quiet conviction, "If I had a gun, Mae, I'd be ready to do it, too."

"Might not be a bad idea, even if you're not fixing to shoot someone," Mae suggested. "Learning how to shoot, I mean."

That was something that had never crossed Kate's mind, although she had admired Jessie's apparent ability to protect herself. She looked thoughtful but did not reply. Instead, she examined Mae's face carefully, realizing fully for the first time how drawn and tired she looked. Mae had been everyone's strength all day.

"Mae," Kate said kindly, "why don't you go and get some rest. I'll wait here for any news."

Mae gaped at her as if she could not believe her ears. "Lord, girl. Do you know where you are? And who I am, for that matter? Your folks'll take a fit when they hear where you spent the afternoon. You can't stay here."

That set look returned to Kate's face. "You helped save Jessie's life—that's what I know about you. And so far, this place suits me fine. Just fine." She placed her hand gently on Mae's and looked resolutely into her eyes. "I'm not going anywhere until we know. Please let me do something, Mae. I can't sit at home and talk about foolishness. Please."

Mae gave in to her tiredness. "All right, honey. But you stay back here away from the bar. The boys are gonna be mean tonight, and I don't want you hearing all that bad talk."

Kate's eyes blazed, and she said bitterly, "Do you think words could bother me after seeing Jessie like that this morning?"

Mae nodded silently. She understood just what Kate was feeling, because she felt the same way. She also wondered if Kate knew what it meant.

Chapter
15

Mae awakened to an insistent rapping on her door.

"Mae, Mae, wake up! The doctor sent word for you to come. Mae!"

She sat up, pulling the ties of her bodice together hastily. "Come in, Kate. I'm awake."

Kate hurried in, her face flushed.

"What time is it?" Mae asked as she hurried about the room, gathering her things and pushing her hair into some kind of order.

"A little before ten."

Mae stared at her. "Lord, girl! Your parents will have the marshal out searching for you."

"No, they won't." Kate shook her head. "I know my father won't go home until there's word from the marshal about the outlaws, so I sent John Emory to tell my mother I was staying in town at the news office."

"There'll be the devil to pay for that tale," Mae said admiringly.

"That may be, but I don't care." Kate held the door open, too anxious to talk any more. "Hurry!"

They rushed down the hall, the sound of the dancehall piano and loud male voices echoing up the stairwell from the bar

below. Behind the closed doors on either side of the narrow cor-
ridor, muted laughter and low moans filtered through the thin
walls. On any other day of her life, Kate would have been
shocked to hear what was happening in those rooms. She didn't
think anything would ever shock her again.

They left through the second floor door to the stairs into the
alley, the same way Kate had come with Jessie their first afternoon together. The streets were strangely empty; many of the
men were still out riding with the marshal's posse. As they
passed the newspaper office, Martin Beecher stepped out,
exclaiming with surprise at the sight of his daughter.

"Kate! What are you doing in town this late?"

"I'm on my way to the doctor's," she explained. "I'll be
home later."

He stared at her, open-mouthed. Kate thought she heard Mae
chuckle faintly beside her.

"But Kate," he protested faintly, "without an escort..."

"Don't worry, Father. I'm fine," she said as she hurried on.

"Wait for me there," he called after them. "I'll take you
home."

As they approached the door to the doctor's office, they
slowed abruptly and stared at each other. Kate's eyes were suddenly wide and frightened. Mae's mouth was set in a grim line.
Reaching out, Mae took Kate's hand.

"Come on, honey. Let's go in."

Kate nodded and together they entered the small anteroom.
The doctor, looking worn out and rumpled, sat behind the scarred
wooden desk. Kate held her breath, waiting for his words like a
sentence of judgment.

"She's better, Mae. Weak, but better."

Kate gave a little gasp and sat down quickly on one of the
hard, straight-backed chairs that lined the wall opposite the doctor. Her limbs suddenly refused to support her.

The doctor continued speaking. "She's not well enough to
move yet, but tomorrow I think we ought to get her over to your
place. Can you look after her there for a while? It'll be a few
days before she's likely to wake up, and the wound'll need tending."

"Sure, Doc," Mae said immediately. "Won't be the first time we've turned a room upstairs into a sickroom."

He nodded as he recalled all the times that Mae had quietly provided a bed, food, and care to some unfortunate with nowhere else to go and received precious little thanks for it, too. He had always thought that Mae was a damn fine woman. Too bad some of the good townspeople didn't think so.

"Doctor," Kate asked, her voice low but steady, "may I see her, please?"

"But she's not awake yet, my dear. She wouldn't know you were there," the doctor replied in a startled voice.

"I don't care about that," Kate insisted. "Just for a moment. Please." Her voice was firm.

"But..." he began.

Mae took a deep breath, thinking how Kate had waited all day, pale and patient and determined. Knowing she'd probably regret it, she commented, "Can't do no harm, can it, Doc?"

He looked from one to the other; each regarded him steadily, their eyes never wavering. *Strange pair, a young society lady and a lady of the evening.* But he'd seen stranger things out here in this godless country, and many things far worse. He decided that he was no match for the two of them together.

"Not more than a minute," he relented. "And don't wake her."

⌘ ❖ ♦ ❖ ♦ ❖ ♦ ⌘

An oil lamp, turned down low and situated in one corner, cast flickering shadows throughout the small windowless room. A single iron bed occupied the center of the narrow space, a straight-backed wooden chair nearby. The sound of low, raspy breathing broke the deep silence. As her eyes adjusted, Kate made out the still shape of Jessie's body beneath the covers. She pulled her lower lip hard between her teeth to stop its trembling and quietly stepped to the side of the bed.

Jessie's eyes were closed, her face pale and impossibly defenseless. A bandage covered the right side of her head, and the sight of a bright spot of blood in its center tore at Kate's heart. She was reminded that Jessie, for all her strength, was vulnerable, too. She watched the slow rise of Jessie's chest beneath the thin blanket and realized how quickly life could change, forever.

She reached out and softly stroked Jessie's cheek. "It's Kate, Jessie," she whispered softly. "You're going to be all right." She lifted Jessie's cool fingers and cradled them in her hand, stroking the work-roughened palm gently. "You must sleep, and get well."

Kate wanted to *make* Jessie well; she wanted to give Jessie her strength and shield her while she healed, but she felt so helpless that her chest ached. Her throat tightened with a longing so intense she had to close her eyes against the pain, drawing comfort from the steady sound of Jessie breathing. Finally, she leaned forward and brushed her lips gently over Jessie's cheek. "Rest now," she whispered.

When she returned to the room where Mae waited with the doctor, Kate said, "I'd like to help you look after her, Mae. You can't possibly do it all yourself."

Mae looked at her steadily for a moment, wanting to refuse, not entirely certain why. "I don't think I could keep you away, could I?" she asked quietly.

"No, Mae. You couldn't."

Mae nodded silently. Some things would have to be settled later.

⌘ ❖ ♦ ❖ ♦ ❖ ♦ ⌘

"Martin, you must forbid it," Martha Beecher began in an agitated voice after Kate had made her announcement and gone up to bed. "You simply have to make Kate see reason. It is just not fitting for her to be spending time in that...that place. And with those women. She has to think of her reputation."

Her husband frowned and replied shortly, "For heaven's sake, Martha, she wants to help take care of a woman who was...uh, injured...saving people's lives." He thought it best not to remind his wife that Jessie Forbes had been shot. Martha was already distraught enough. "No one is going to think anything evil about Kate for that."

Martha was hurt by the harsh tone in his voice, and tears came to her eyes. "I'm only thinking of Kate."

"I know you are, dear." Martin went to his wife and put his hands on her shoulders. "But you must try to understand. Life is hard, and women out here need to be different. All of us must do things we never had to do before. Kate understands that. She is doing the proper thing."

She looked at him, clearly unconvinced. "What she *needs* is to be settled and safe. I'm not at all sure that this place is good for her. Not sure at all."

He sighed. "This isn't the usual situation, Martha. I'm sure that Kate will fine. You said yourself that you liked Ken Turner."

Martha rested her head on his shoulder, her anger draining away. "Oh Martin, I truly am so worried about her. She seems to have changed somehow since we came here. I feel as if I hardly know her."

He smoothed her hair, holding her carefully. "Kate is a good child, Martha. Let's give her a little time, and if you still feel she's not on the proper course, we'll talk about what needs to be done. I'm sure that you know what's best for her."

She nodded, wishing fervently that Kate had stayed behind in Boston.

Chapter
16

For a long time there was a horrible pain somewhere inside her, and when it began, her mind retreated. She slept. While she slept, she dreamed. She wandered over vast barren prairies and through dark mountain passes, searching for a place to rest. Each time she stopped, she waited, lonely and so cold, for the comfort that never came.

She drifted in and out of consciousness, dimly aware that she was not alone. Soft voices soothed her, and softer hands placed cool cloths on her burning forehead, bathing the fever from her skin. Gentle, insistent hands held her and forced nourishment between her lips. She struggled less and less with each touch, letting herself be healed. In the end, it was hunger that woke her.

Opening her eyes, Jessie turned her face slowly toward the raised window. She blinked against the first assault of sunlight, even as she welcomed the banishment of the dark that had surrounded her for so long. A breeze gently fluttered the curtains. Kate was sitting before the window, a book open in her lap.

Jessie lay silent for a moment, studying her. She didn't appear to be reading, but stared down into the street, her expression distant. Wisps of black hair, too thick to be contained, framed her face. Her full lips were unsmiling, and there were dark smudges under her eyes. She looked worn and weary, seeming older than Jessie remembered. Even though Kate was clearly exhausted, Jessie thought her beautiful.

"How long have you been here, Kate?" Jessie asked quietly.

Kate gave a startled cry, turning to Jessie, her eyes wide. What she saw was what she had prayed for, every moment of the endless days since the wagon had carried Jessie into town—' Jessie, her deep blue eyes clear and strong; Jessie, perfect lips curled into a faint smile of greeting. *Jessie.* The resolve that had sustained Kate through near sleepless nights and days of worry dissolved with the swift rush of relief, and tears sprang to her eyes. She whispered Jessie's name, holding herself tightly, and cried.

Jessie waited for the storm to pass, wishing she could comfort her, but she didn't think she could walk that far. "Kate," she said gently as Kate's quiet sobs abated. She made one feeble attempt to sit up but quickly abandoned the idea when a searing pain ran down her arm. She gritted her teeth for a moment, then tried again. "Kate."

Swiping at the tears on her cheek, Kate came to Jessie's side, smiling tremulously. "Don't try to get up. You've been...shot, Jessie." Just saying the words caused her stomach to clench with a fresh surge of anxiety and fear.

"Don't worry," Jessie gasped, watching the concern flicker across Kate's face. Leaning back on the pillow, she quickly assured her, "I'll save getting out of bed for a bit later."

Kate touched Jessie's hand, stroking it softly. "What you need to do is sleep."

"That's all I've *been* doing, seems like," Jessie protested feebly as she threaded her fingers through Kate's. She tried a valiant smile, but the throbbing in her shoulder was making it hard for her to think clearly. She closed her eyes against the pain and murmured, "If you could just stay another minute..."

"I can stay as long as you need me," Kate whispered, watching her drift off.

When Jessie opened her eyes again, Kate was still close by, having pulled the chair up to the bedside. It was dark outside the window now.

"Same day?" Jessie asked.

"Yes," Kate said with a smile. "Feeling better?"

"Some," Jessie acknowledged. She was grateful for even the temporary cessation of the worst of the ache. "What happened with those bastards who held up the stage? Did I at least get one of 'em, do you know?"

"Yes," Kate replied, wondering how Jessie could be so calm. She wondered also at herself, discussing something she had never even imagined before. During the torturous hours of waiting, not knowing if Jessie would recover, she had come to realize that she was a far different woman now than the sheltered young girl of less than a year ago. She had found an inner strength she might never have known had she not come to this wild and dangerous place, had she not met this fierce yet so gentle woman. "You saved lives, Jessie. I'm so proud of you."

"No," Jessie said quickly, blushing at the praise. "Anyone would have done the same. I just happened to be there."

Kate smiled at her clear discomfort. "You say that, but I don't think so."

"You look tired, Kate," Jessie remarked, hoping to change the subject but also concerned about the shadows under the other woman's eyes.

"Oh, I must look a fright," Kate said, suddenly self-conscious, as she brushed her hair back. But the heavy locks would not be tamed.

"No," Jessie said seriously. "You're beautiful."

Kate colored slightly, but her eyes shone with pleasure. She asked tenderly, "Are you in pain, Jessie?"

The rancher forced a grin. "Not as bad as the time the bull ran me down when I was ten." She held Kate's eyes for a long moment, marveling at their dark beauty, and quickly forgot the throbbing in her shoulder. "How long have I been here?" she asked at last.

"Almost a week." *It seemed forever,* Kate thought.

During that week, she and Mae and several of Mae's girls had taken turns sitting by Jessie's bed, changing her nightshirt when she soaked it through with sweat, replacing the bloody bandages and cleaning the terrible wounds, forcing her to drink,

and soothing her when she had cried out in the throes of some
dream terror. Kate had come every day, despite her mother's
increasingly vocal objections, and she often sent the others
away, preferring to look after Jessie herself. All except Mae.

Mae would often come in when Kate was there, to simply
stand at the foot of the bed and watch Jessie sleep. When she was
satisfied that Jessie was all right, she would disappear into the
night. Where she went and what she did were none of Kate's
affair, although Kate was fairly sure that she knew precisely
what Mae was doing, and she found that she didn't care. Jessie
had almost been killed. Realizing that if it hadn't been a gunshot
it might have been a stampeding horse or a rockslide up in the
hills, Kate suddenly had a new appreciation of what truly mat-
tered in life, and it certainly wasn't judging what someone else
did to survive.

"The doctor says you'll be fine, but you need to rest," Kate
assured her.

"Damn, I feel weak as a kitten." Jessie frowned. "And I'm
not going to get any stronger lying up here." She tried again to
push herself up. A wave of dizziness rolled over her, followed
quickly by a fierce surge of pain. She groaned and struggled not
to faint.

Kate reached for her without thinking, moving onto the edge
of the bed and supporting Jessie's shivering body against her
side with a protective arm around her shoulders. Holding Jessie's
face to her breast, she stroked the damp hair back from her forehead. Jessie trembled. Kate caught her breath as something
turned over inside of her, and with an effort, she said quietly,
"You can't get up. Not just yet."

Jessie relaxed into the soft warmth, too weak to protest, and
Kate just held her. Kate had never been this close to another
human being before, other than her parents. Nothing she had
ever imagined had prepared her for the wave of tenderness that
swept through her. She could scarcely breathe.

"Well," Mae said acerbically from the doorway behind
them. "I guess our patient's getting better." She carried a tray to
the dresser before turning to the women on the bed. *They're
looking mighty cozy.*

Kate released Jessie gently and stepped quietly to one side. She met Mae's eyes squarely but could not read the expression in her cool green gaze. Then Mae looked away from her toward the woman on the bed, and her face softened.

"How are you, Montana?" she asked, her voice husky. "It sure is good to see you with your eyes open."

Jessie worked up a smile. "I'm downright embarrassed, Mae. Letting a couple of no-goods get the best of me and causing all this trouble."

Mae smiled fondly. "Jess, the only trouble you would have caused is if you'd up and died on us."

"I'm sorry, but I can't seem to stay awake," Jessie complained feebly. She grinned a little sheepishly, but the pain had taken its toll.

A hint of challenge in her eyes, Mae turned to Kate. "I suspect Jess needs to rest a bit."

"Yes," Kate answered slowly. She couldn't bear the thought of leaving, but Mae looked ready to argue and that would only upset Jessie. "I think we should *both* go and let her sleep."

⌘ ❖ ♦ ❖ ♦ ❖ ♦ ⌘

Jessie awakened the following day to discover that the sun was already high in the sky, and she had lost nearly another day. She didn't mind so much when she found that she was not alone.

"What is that you're reading, Kate?" she asked, managing to sit up this time with much less pain.

"The sonnets of Mr. William Shakespeare." Kate placed her finger on the page and lightly closed the cover on the leather-bound book. She looked across the room at Jessie and was heartened to see how much better she appeared. There was color in her face and a sparkle in her eyes that Kate had feared she might never see again. "Do you know them?"

"I've heard of *him*, but I'm not much for poetry. I'd rather have a story, I guess."

"Every time I read one of his sonnets," Kate said, smiling, "I find something new to enjoy, even though I know most of them by heart."

Seriously contemplating Kate's words, Jessie nodded. Finally she ventured, "Like always being surprised at how pretty the sunset is, even after seeing a thousand of them."

"Yes," Kate said quietly, her gaze meeting Jessie's tenderly, "exactly like that."

Jessie flushed, having never known such quiet communion in the rough world of cowboys. For some unknown reason, it did funny things to her breathing, and it wasn't from something broken, but from something right.

Kate's hands trembled as they held tightly to the thin volume in her lap, knowing that Jessie saw her as no one else ever had. To others, she had always been just another young woman with her future predetermined by virtue of her sex and status. Her father had allowed her to be different than other young girls, but only to a point. She might read in the college library, but he had not suggested she attend classes there. Jessie seemed content to let her simply be. The silence grew heavy as their eyes held, two women united not by common experience but by a common sensitivity that drew them together more surely than convention or class.

Eventually, comforted in body and soul, Jessie closed her eyes and slept again. Kate, her heart full, smiled and returned to her book of poems.

Chapter
17

Jessie pulled the window curtain aside, looking down the street for her for the sixth time in as many minutes. It was well past the time that Kate usually arrived in the morning, and Jessie was starting to worry. It was only a mile or so from Kate's home into town, and almost the entire route was well populated, but still, she was a woman out alone. Ordinarily, Jessie wouldn't have been so anxious, but her nerves were jangling as she considered what she was about to do.

"Well, you're up and dressed awfully early," a voice behind her observed.

Jessie turned. Mae stood just inside the door, still in her dressing gown. "I want to go home, Mae," Jessie said without preamble.

"Now Jess," Mae said, working to keep her voice even, "the doc said you couldn't ride yet. You know darn well if you go back to the Rising Star that's the first thing you'll want to do."

Jessie leaned against the window and muttered under her breath. Her face was thinner, but her color had returned. "Mae, I just can't stand it anymore. Lord knows what's going on out there. Jed is a good man, and I know it. But that's *my* ranch." The distraught rancher paced the room impatiently, frowning. "I just won't be right until I get out into the air again—out of town."

"It won't be much longer, Jess," Mae tried again. *Lord, you can't tell these cowboys anything!* "If you open up that tear in your shoulder, you could be in real trouble."

"Mae, I swear," Jessie fumed, pushing her hands into the pockets of her levis. "I just don't feel healthy in here. And as kind as you've been, I feel like I'm fettered."

Laughing, Mae went to her and lightly gripped her tense shoulders. She had to stand on tiptoe to look into those blue eyes, and she leaned against Jessie lightly for support. She shook her head, smiling at the perplexed expression she found in Jessie's eyes. "Oh, I know you're grateful, Montana. And I know just what you're feeling. I've known a lot of cowboys in my time, and I learned better than to try to tame one. But if you go, you'd better promise to look after yourself. You ain't seen nothing 'til you've seen me mad."

"I *have* seen you mad, and believe me, I don't want to chance it. It's my shoulder that's ailing, not my head." Jessie smiled down at Mae and gently encircled her waist. She held the shorter woman fondly as she said, "I want to thank you, Mae, for everything you've done for me. I know how bad off I was, and I owe you my life, I guess."

"I had help," Mae acknowledged as she tilted her head back and searched Jessie's face. Suddenly serious, she said softly, "Something special would have gone out of my life if I lost you, Jess." She pressed closer, sliding her arms around Jessie's neck, and put her lips gently on Jessie's mouth. She'd meant it innocently enough, but the feel of their bodies together brought a low moan from Mae's throat. Her fingers slipped into the thick hair at Jessie's nape as she came dangerously close to kissing her like she'd always wanted to.

"Oh, my!" Kate cried in surprise as she pushed open the door. She stared, speechless, at Jessie holding Mae in her arms.

Wordlessly, Jessie looked up, quietly releasing Mae. The kiss had taken her by surprise, and she was momentarily stunned by the softness of Mae's lips. She remembered dreaming, that night in the bath, of kissing lips as soft as those. But it had not been Mae she had dreamed of then, and with a hint of relief, she said, "Why, Kate. Come in."

"I'm sorry. I should have knocked," Kate said coolly, rapidly composing herself. Her first flush of embarrassment at coming upon such an intimate scene was quickly replaced by something else. She wasn't sure why, but the sight of Mae in Jessie's arms made her angry.

Jessie smiled, innocently pleased to see her at last, the kiss already forgotten. "I've been wondering where you were."

Confused, Kate stared from one to the other of them, chiding herself for making too much of what she had just witnessed. Jessie's greeting to her was warm and welcoming, the way it always was. But a feeling of disquiet still lingered. Her heart pounding, trying to appear unperturbed, she answered, "Hello, Jessie. Hi, Mae."

Mae stepped slowly away from Jessie, turning toward Kate with an enigmatic smile. "Yes, Kate. Do come in. I was just...uh, saying goodbye to Montana here."

"Goodbye?" Kate cried, her anger forgotten. She had consciously avoided thinking about what would happen when Jessie was healed, because she knew that Jessie would leave. Then, Kate feared, she would be left as she had been before, alone in a life she found increasingly oppressive. Her heart sinking, she repeated softly, "Goodbye."

Mae touched Jessie lightly on the arm as she headed for the door. "Don't forget to come calling now, Jess."

When they were alone, Kate glared at Jessie, who was awkwardly trying to strap on her gun belt without using her injured arm. "What are you doing?" she asked, fear making her tone sharper than she intended.

Jessie met her eyes in surprise. "Well, I'm going home, Kate."

Putting the parcel of books and basket of food she had been carrying on the dresser, Kate crossed to her. "It's too soon. You'll hurt yourself," she admonished, struggling not to raise her voice.

Jessie held up a hand when she saw the frown on Kate's face. "Now don't you go at me, too. Jed is coming in the buck-

board so I won't have to ride. I've already promised I'll be careful."

"You haven't been out of bed but for a day," Kate said
softly, reaching around Jessie's waist with both arms to settle the
wide holster on Jessie's narrow hips. She stood close to her,
threading the worn tongue through the silver buckle, fumbling
slightly with the clasp.

Jessie went very still as Kate worked, acutely aware of
Kate's fingers brushing over her legs. Kate's hair smelled fresh,
like flower petals ripe with spring pollen.

"I promise to lie low when I get home," Jessie insisted. "But
I need to get home."

"How does this thing tie?" Kate asked, her head bent as she
studied the thong hanging from the holster.

"Around my leg," Jessie answered a bit hoarsely. She was
starting to shake, but she didn't feel ill. She stiffened as Kate's
hands encircled her thigh. She felt again as she had in the dream,
stirred deep inside. The intimacy of it was frightening and exhil-
arating all at once.

"Oh," she murmured in surprise as swift heat hit her in the
stomach. Suddenly unsteady, she placed her good hand on Kate's
shoulder to keep her balance. "Kate," she breathed uncertainly.
Lord, what's happening?

Kate stood quickly, reaching for her. Jessie's hands came
around her waist. They stood, a whisper apart, while the room
and reality receded, leaving only the two of them in a place out
of time. Jessie leaned her forehead to Kate's and closed her eyes,
content to rest. Kate rubbed her palms gently up and down
Jessie's back, liking the hard strength of her. Somewhere out in
the hall a woman laughed.

"You're not well yet, Jessie," Kate whispered, her lips close
to Jessie's cheek. She felt their bodies touch, all along her front,
and the room became unbearably warm.

"I know," Jessie conceded, her voice trembling. "But I will
be, Kate. I promise."

Kate sighed, half in anger and half in exasperation. She
leaned back in the circle of Jessie's arms, her dark eyes probing
those astonishing blue ones. She took a step back when she saw

that the decision was made, breaking their embrace. "Jessie Forbes, you are the most stubborn woman I have ever met."

"Thank you," Jessie said, a grin flickering at the corner of her mouth. Now that there was distance between them, her head cleared, and she moved to the side of the bed where her valise stood open.

"It's not funny," Kate snapped, but she couldn't look at her and hold onto her anger. She thought Jessie was never more attractive than she was now, leaning against the bedpost, her arms folded across her chest, one leg crossed in front of the other, all leather and worn denim and cocksureness. Kate felt her face grow hot, and she knew Jessie saw it.

Jessie recognized the lingering blaze of anger in Kate's eyes, but she saw the worry there, too. Seriously, she asked, "What is it, Kate? Have I done something to upset you?"

"I just can't bear to see you hurt again," Kate whispered, tears unexpectedly close to the surface. The memory of Jessie lying motionless, so pale and helpless, was still too fresh in her mind. "Will you be careful, Jessie? Please?"

"Of course," Jessie answered softly. She closed the satchel and lifted it in her right hand, wishing she could erase the unhappiness that still clouded Kate's face. "Come visit, Kate," she said suddenly, realizing that she didn't want to say goodbye. The best thing about being here in town had been seeing Kate every day and the peaceful hours they had spent just quietly talking. For the first time, it occurred to her how lonely the ranch would be now. "Come out to the ranch one day soon."

Kate smiled. "You did promise me a tour." The glow Jessie's suggestion had brought to her eyes disappeared just as quickly. "But it's an hour's ride away, isn't it?"

Jessie nodded again. "Less on a good horse, but you'll need a buckboard. You can have John Emory bring you around. He's always itching to spend time with Jed and the boys. I don't imagine he'd need much prompting."

"I will," Kate affirmed, thinking that her parents would not object to John Emory taking her out for a drive. "This week?"

"Yes," Jessie said as she walked to the door. As an afterthought, she added, "Will you do something for me, Kate?"

Kate waited breathlessly, feeling in that moment that Jessie could ask her anything and she would agree. "You know I will, Jessie."

"It's Mae."

"Mae?" Kate echoed, not understanding.

"You're the only friend, besides me, that Mae really has in this town. The saloon girls look to her for help more often than the other way around, and I expect it gets hard for her...and lonely. I don't get by nearly enough with all I have to do out at the ranch. Will you look in on her now and then?"

"Of course I will, Jessie," Kate promised, wondering if she and Mae were friends after all.

Chapter
18

Jessie sat on her front porch, her boots up on the rail, oiling the stock of her rifle with more vigor than it required. Across the yard, Jed and several of the men were cutting tree lengths for fence posts. She watched them work, feeling useless and out of sorts, muttering colorfully to herself about foremen who didn't have an ounce of respect.

Jed had finally lost his temper after the third time he had to take the saw away from her and told her he was sorry he ever went to pick her up. "Would've left you there in that damn hotel, if I'da known you'd be this much trouble to have around," he had complained. "You won't be worth nothing the rest of the year if you don't let that shoulder heal. And I don't plan on doin' your share of the work forever, so just let that damn saw be."

She knew that he was right, but after three days at home, she was chafing under the weight of inactivity. She had worked every day of her life in some capacity, with the exception of Sundays, when even nonbelievers took a few hours' rest. And there was work to be done now, but most of it required physical strength, which left her sitting on her porch or pacing a path outside the corrals, watching the hands work *her* horses.

Jessie saw the clouds of dust before she heard the clatter of wheels on the road to her house. On her feet in an instant, she leaned over the porch rail, straining to make out the driver and passenger. When she saw who it was, she bounded down the steps to meet the buckboard pulling up in her yard.

"Kate," she cried, walking alongside the wagon, gazing up at Kate in undisguised delight. "You've come."

While John Emory slowed the team to a halt, Kate looked down from her perch on the high seat, almost too happy for words. She forgot completely the struggle she had had with her parents to get permission for John Emory to take her about in the buckboard. To be entirely proper, the two of them should have been chaperoned, but even Martha acknowledged that no one in town would object to the Schroeder boy escorting Kate for her own safety. And since Kate insisted that she needed the buckboard to carry her camera while visiting some of her new friends who lived outside of town, her parents had agreed to the arrangement. It had taken very little convincing to get John Emory to take her to Jessie's ranch.

"You look wonderful," Kate said, pleased to see the healthy color in Jessie's face. "How are you?"

Jessie grinned and reached up as Kate stepped onto the running board to climb down. She wasn't thinking about her shoulder. She didn't seem to be able to think of much of anything else beyond Kate when they were together. "I'm better now. Let me get you down from there."

Kate frowned, placing one hand on Jessie's right shoulder to steady herself, holding her skirt up with the other. "You can't lift me. Let John."

Slipping her right arm around Kate's waist, Jessie merely laughed and pulled Kate into her arms, supporting most of the young woman's weight on the side away from her injured shoulder. She held her for just a moment, surprised by Kate's firm suppleness. Then she gently released her. "I'm fine," she repeated, her eyes on Kate's flushed face. *I really do feel much better when you're near.*

She looked at John Emory, who had jumped down and was standing by the back of the wagon, hands stuffed in the pockets of his trousers, looking uncertain. "Jed's over in the corral behind the main barn with some of the men. Why don't you go on over?"

"Sure thing, Jessie," he exclaimed, looking relieved. "I'll be back in a bit, Kate," he added as he hurried away.

Kate nodded, unable to take her eyes from Jessie, who wasn't wearing her usual workday vest and chaps. The levis and soft cotton shirt accentuated her slender body. Kate knew very well what Jessie's body looked like under those clothes, but for the first time she was thinking of her not as a patient but as a vital, attractive woman. Realizing that she was staring, Kate said shyly, "It's so good to see you."

"Yes," Jessie replied, finding it hard to do anything but look in return. Finally, she asked, "Would you like to walk around a little? See the ranch?"

Kate slipped her hand through Jessie's arm. "Oh, yes. Please." Almost as an afterthought, she added, "And I was hoping that you could teach me how to drive the buckboard, too."

Jessie stopped dead. "The buckboard?"

"I can't very well drag John Emory out here every time I want to come visiting, now can I?"

"Well, you can't drive out here alone, either, especially unarmed," Jessie said with finality. She walked toward the horse barns as if the matter were settled.

"Well, I thought I'd save the shooting lessons until the next visit," Kate remarked calmly.

Jessie glanced at her quickly, saw the look of determination, and grinned. "We'll let your hands heal from the blisters you're gonna get handling that team before we start in with the Winchester."

Kate nodded. "That's sounds quite reasonable." Then she smiled, an excited smile so brilliant that Jessie was momentarily lost.

Regaining a bit of composure, she announced, "I'll show you the brood mares down at the corral, then we'll take the buckboard out to the north pasture where the yearlings are summering. Don't see why you can't drive out there."

When at length they returned to the shade of Jessie's porch, cool drinks in hand, Kate had seen most of the Rising Star ranch within easy riding distance of the house. She had also discovered

that driving the buckboard was quite a bit easier than controlling
the heavy wagon in which she and her family had traveled west.
There had been times during the trip when her father had needed
to lever the wagon's wheels from some mud-laden trench or to
lead the horses by hand through a dangerous stretch, and Kate
had taken the reins. She had loved the excitement of handling the
team then, and she loved the freedom that it would give her now.

"Try this," Jessie said, handing Kate a tin of some thick yellow salve that smelled surprisingly like honey.

"It's so peaceful here," Kate remarked, smearing the oint-
ment over the sore spots on her palms. Jessie's gloves had pro-
tected her some, but she wouldn't want her mother to see these
blisters. She placed the tin on the rail and surveyed the rising
expanse of hills that climbed steeply toward the mountains edg-
ing the horizon. A stream flowed in a ribbon of blue across the
golden brown flatland. The gently undulating plains were
marked here and there by patches of greener grass and clusters of
trees.

As she turned her head, she caught sight of Jessie's face in
profile. She thought how much Jessie was like her land, bold and
strong and sure. "Beautiful."

Jessie nodded. "Yes."

"Do you ever get lonely?" Kate asked, wondering if perhaps
she were the only one who longed for something more.

Jessie met her questioning gaze. "Sometimes," she said quietly. "Sometimes I miss you."

Kate smiled, feeling far, far less alone.

⌘ ❖ ♦ ❖ ♦ ❖ ♦ ⌘

As the days passed, Jessie's strength returned. Her shoulder
healed, and she could finally ride again. From sunup to sundown,
she kept busy with the ever-present demands of the ranch, but
when evening came, she stood on the porch surrounded by
silence, feeling the disappointment of another day when Kate
had not come. Sleep remained an elusive respite, and she grew
weary in body and soul.

Early one afternoon, she decided to survey the creek where

she meant to build a dam. There was a small hollow between two wooded knolls that would make a fine natural shelter for the animals to winter. All it needed was water. The day was warm, and she let Star have her head, riding low over her neck as they flew across the countryside. Nearing the hill overlooking the gully, she saw figures moving under the trees. Rustlers were not uncommon, and she approached slowly, one hand casually on her gun belt.

Kate had been watching the rider race across the flatlands, and she knew long before she could see her face that it was Jessie. She couldn't mistake her lean figure or graceful seat on the galloping horse for anyone else. As Jessie drew closer, Kate saw the wary tension in her face. Ken Turner napped contentedly beside her, lulled to sleep by the effects of a hearty lunch and the warm sun. She placed her hand gently on his shoulder and shook him as Jessie rode up to them.

"Jessie," Kate cried, elated to see her. She had tried for days to convince her father to let her take the buckboard out alone, but all her arguing had been to no avail. She wanted desperately to visit Jessie again, but John Emory had been needed at the newspaper office and could not accompany her.

To complete her frustration, she could no longer politely refuse Ken Turner's repeated invitations for an afternoon drive, especially when her mother kept urging her to accept. So finally she found herself in the only place she wanted to be—on the Rising Star ranch—with precisely the wrong person. It had been agony sitting for hours with Ken Turner, making casual conversation and feigning interest in the attorney's self-important plans, while all the time her mind was on Jessie. *And now she's here.*

"It's so good to see you. Mr. Turner and I were just having lunch. Come join us."

"No. No thank you, Kate," Jessie replied, her voice tight as she looked at the man slowly sitting up. Her glance quickly surveyed the picnic basket and Kate's hand on Ken's shoulder, and she flushed. "I'm sorry, I didn't mean to bother you. I didn't know who you were at first."

Ken, awake now, smiled in a rather superior way. "Oh, not

at all, Miss Forbes. After all, we are trespassing, so to speak."
He slipped his arm possessively around Kate's waist, looking for
all the world like a man content with himself, and posturing as if
Kate were already his.

Jessie stared at him coldly, her eyes impenetrable. "Kate is
always welcome on my land. I think she knows that." She tipped
her hat slightly to Kate and said tersely, "Good day then."

Before Kate could answer, Jessie whirled Star around and
galloped away. Kate shook off Ken's arm, staring after the rapidly retreating figure, her heart sinking. She had wanted so much
to see her, and now she had hurt her. That was the last thing she
had ever meant to do. She barely heard Ken as he informed her
that he had news of some import to discuss. All she could hear
was the receding thunder of hooves and the fading jingle of
spurs.

Chapter
19

That evening, sitting with Ken Turner and her parents in the parlor, Kate was especially uneasy. Ken's polite but proprietary manner was becoming more difficult to bear, and his subtle but persistent caresses harder to avoid. The longer she spent trying to act as if nothing were wrong, the more certain she became that she needed to make a decision. Something must be done, but she couldn't help but feel that there was something vital she did not understand. When she could bear the social pleasantries and forced cheeriness no longer, she pleaded a headache and escaped to the quiet of her room.

Now she lay staring into the darkness, struggling to understand her feelings. It had been agony not to see Jessie these past weeks. To finally see her that afternoon without being able to say how much she had missed her was even worse. The pain in Jessie's eyes haunted her. When she'd ridden away, Kate had feared that her own heart might break. She needed someone to talk to; she needed help. And she knew of only one place to go.

⌘ ❖ ♦ ❖ ♦ ❖ ♦ ⌘

Kate hesitated outside Mae's door, her confidence suddenly waning. When she had awakened early after a restless night, it had seemed so clear to her. Now that she was here, she wasn't so certain anymore. Finally, she forced herself to knock.

"Kate!" Mae said with surprise after answering the tap on her door. The sun had barely risen, and since she kept late hours, she had only just been to bed. She tied her robe and gestured Kate into her room. "What is it?"

"Can I talk with you, Mae?" Kate asked, standing awkwardly just inside the door. She had never been in Mae's bedroom before, and the sudden intimacy of the moment embarrassed her.

"Of course," Mae replied, gesturing to two chairs on either side of a small dressing table. "Sit down."

Kate sat quickly, afraid that she might suddenly lose her resolve and run. Mae's sharp eyes took in the tremor in Kate's hands and the uneasiness in her expression. She pulled a chair close.

"What *is* it, Kate?" she asked softly.

Tears brimmed behind Kate's lashes. "Mae, Ken Turner intends to speak to my father about marriage."

Mae looked at her intently, not particularly surprised. There wasn't much going on around town that she didn't eventually hear about. She had hoped that the rumors about Turner and Kate were true and that there was a match in the making. But looking at Kate now, she began to doubt it. "You don't look too happy about it. I always thought that's what a girl like you would want. I should think he'd make a good catch, well-respected and responsible, and all that."

"Oh, you're quite right," Kate said, bitterly. "He *is* a fine man, and I have nothing against him. But..." Her voice trailed off, and she struggled for the words.

"But what, honey?" Mae asked gently.

"I don't love him."

Mae laughed, although there was an edge to it. "Do you think you'll be the first woman to make a good match with a man she doesn't love? If he provides for you and doesn't mistreat you or disgrace you, you may find after a while that you love him. The heart does funny things, sometimes. And if not, you'll be no different than a lot of other women and better off than many."

"I don't want to spend my life with someone I don't love," Kate insisted.

Mae eyed her sharply. "Love doesn't put a roof over your head, Kate, or feed you, or earn you respect from your neighbors. I know."

"I won't marry him just for that," Kate said with finality.

"Then wait for a fella more to your choosing," Mae acquiesced, having heard that stubborn tone in Kate's voice before. "You're young yet."

Kate looked at Mae and asked in a low voice, "What if...what if there's someone else?"

Mae had been expecting something like this, but the girl's honesty surprised her. "Is there someone else, Kate?"

Kate nodded slowly, relief softening her tense features. "Yes."

"Who is it?" Mae asked, needing to hear the words. Maybe she was wrong. Because if she wasn't, she didn't know quite what she would say.

"Jessie."

Mae sighed, closing her eyes briefly. When she opened them, Kate was staring intently at her. "So it's Jessie, is it?"

"Yes," Kate answered, her voice filled with sudden wonder. "Yes. Yes, Mae. I love Jessie." After so many weeks of not seeing, of being so close but not knowing, saying the words made everything clear. Now she understood why she felt so lonely and lost whenever they parted, and why she lay awake at night searching for ways to see her again. *It's Jessie who makes me feel special and cared for. It's Jessie who makes my spirit soar and my heart lift with happiness. It's Jessie I love.*

"I've been wondering if you'd ever figure that out," Mae said quietly.

Kate drew a surprised breath and looked at Mae questioningly. "You knew?"

Mae laughed darkly. "I was pretty sure. But I was hoping you wouldn't keep on, that you'd marry your Mr. Turner and settle down the way you should."

"But why, Mae?" Kate asked, hearing Mae's opposition but still not comprehending it. *How could it be bad when what I feel for Jessie seems so right?*

"Why? Because of Jessie, for Lord's sake." Kate's obvious naiveté finally ignited Mae's anger. She got quickly to her feet, seething. "You say that you love her. She'll love you, too, you know. Probably already does. Do you have any idea what that's going to do to her?"

"Mae, I..." Kate stared at her, stunned by the vehemence in her voice.

"Jessie's been waiting her whole life for this, and she doesn't even know it," Mae continued as if she hadn't heard. "You'll let her believe, Kate, and then you'll leave her, sooner or later. That will destroy her."

"No!" Kate cried passionately. "I won't hurt her. I couldn't hurt her. Believe me, Mae, I won't change."

Looking at her silently, Mae was uncertain whether to go on. But Kate had come to her, and there might not be another time. "Kate, you're young. When you're young, blood runs high. I believe you've got feelings for her. I do." She took a breath. "But *think* what you're saying. If you let Jessie love you, how long do you think it will be before Jessie wants to love you like...like...a man loves a woman?"

Kate felt her face redden, but she would not avert her gaze. She thought about the way her heart raced when Jessie was near, the way her breath tripped when she looked into Jessie's eyes, and the way she trembled at the barest touch of Jessie's hand. She envisioned Jessie, sweat-dampened and dusty and so incredibly beautiful, and she was suddenly warm all over. She *knew* what she felt. She studied Mae calmly, her face composed. "And you, Mae. Could you love her like that?"

"I would now, if she'd let me." Mae's expression was proud, but her eyes were sad.

Kate nodded slowly and rose. She touched Mae's arm lightly as she left. "Thank you."

Mae looked after her, admiring her grit, and praying that she'd come to her senses before it was too late.

Chapter
20

Jessie came around the side of the barn, stopped abruptly, and stared. A buckboard was pulled up in her yard, and it looked a lot like Kate standing on her front porch. It had been only a day or two since she had seen Kate with that Turner fellow out on the range, and she hadn't wanted to think too long about what that meant. In fact, she had been working harder than ever just so she *wouldn't* have to think about it. But she still recalled his arm around Kate's waist, like he owned her, and just remembering it made her want to curse. She had been afraid that Kate might never visit again, and now, here she was. Jessie broke into a run and took the stairs two at a time.

"Kate?" she said in astonishment. She couldn't keep the note of elation from her voice.

Kate smiled at her. "Hello, Jessie."

Jessie looked perplexed. "What are you doing here?" She looked around the ranch. "Where's John Emory?"

"He isn't here. I came by myself." Kate wanted to laugh at the open amazement on Jessie's face, but she took note of the flicker of worry that lingered there as well and added quietly, "I needed to see you."

"Come inside," Jessie said, holding the door for her. "It's too hot out here already, and it isn't even noon."

Kate carried the basket she had packed and stepped into the cool dark hallway. She waited for Jessie to lead the way, following her through to the library.

As soon as they were seated in the two leather chairs facing the empty fireplace, Jessie asked, "How did you ever get your parents to let you come?"

"They think that I'm at the Schroeder's, helping Hannah."

Jessie looked shocked. "Lord, Kate."

Finally, Kate laughed. She was so glad to see her. "They don't expect me home until tonight, and I just couldn't wait until John Emory had the time to bring me."

"What's so important?" Jessie asked, her blue eyes clouded with concern. "Has something happened?"

"Last night Ken Turner asked me to marry him," Kate said quietly.

"Oh." Jessie felt as if she had been struck. She stood up quickly and paced to the fireplace, needing distance. Some hard deep pain was threatening to break loose inside her, and she wanted to run. She wanted to be alone, because she didn't think she'd be able to weather this news in Kate's presence. Willing her legs to stay in place, she closed her eyes for just a minute, trying to get her bearings. She was having a little trouble catching her breath. She tried to swallow around the lump in her throat, but her voice came out choked. "I...that's grand, Kate," she managed.

Kate went to her side, placing her hand on Jessie's arm. She felt Jessie trembling, and it brought tears to her eyes. "It's not what you think, Jessie," she said softly. "I told him no."

Jessie stared at Kate, her expression desolate. Her mind swirled with confusion. All she could think was that Kate would be gone. "I don't understand," she whispered.

"I told him no, Jessie," Kate murmured, very close to her now, "because it's you I love."

A strange pounding began in Jessie's chest. Kate's words suddenly set her world straight. All the restless yearnings that had plagued her these past weeks vanished like mist in the sunlight. She wanted to say and do a thousand things, but all she could manage was to look into Kate's eyes. They were so dark, so warm, and so welcoming.

"Kate," she breathed, her voice low, "I...I don't know what to say. I...I'm—"

Kate touched her fingers to Jessie's lips, silencing her gently. "I don't want you to say anything, Jessie." She laid her cheek against Jessie's shoulder, threading her arms around Jessie's waist. "I just want you to hold me."

A soft sigh escaped Jessie's lips. She stood very still, feeling Kate against every inch of her body, the blood rushing hot through her veins. She rested her trembling hands on Kate's waist, marveling at her softness. Very slowly, afraid that Kate might step away, she brushed her face over Kate's thick hair, closing her eyes as the sweet fragrance engulfed her. The sensation was too much to bear, and she groaned faintly.

Kate listened to the beat of Jessie's heart as contentment warred with something much more urgent—a swift stab of pleasure that bordered on pain. "Oh," she murmured, pressing harder to Jessie.

"What is it?" Jessie asked hoarsely, her throat tight with emotion. So many feelings assaulted her she couldn't think. Holding Kate in her arms, she felt a mixture of tenderness and longing so fierce she ached. "Kate, what's wrong?"

At last, Kate lifted her head to look at Jessie's face and found her expression ravenous, almost wild. Kate forgot to breathe for a long moment. "I don't know," she gasped at last. "I want...oh, Jessie. I don't know what I want." As she spoke, she steadily stroked Jessie's back, her shoulders, her chest—needing to feel her, wanting to get closer to her. She wasn't aware of anything save a craving more critical than anything she had ever known. "I think about you," she murmured, pushing her fingers into Jessie's hair, pulling the taller woman's head closer to her own. "I think about you...touching me."

Jessie was sure she was about to die. Her heart hammered in her chest, her lungs burned, and her legs threatened to give out. Her hands tightened on Kate's body, pulling her close, wanting her near, needing to tell Kate with every fiber of her being how much she needed her. How much she loved her. She had no words, but her heart knew. She dipped her head, closing that final distance between them, and pressed her lips gently to Kate's, letting the soft certainty of her kiss speak for her.

Kate's lips parted initially in surprise, then in wonder. Jessie's kiss, tender at first, became more possessive, and Kate swayed in Jessie's arms as heat hummed through her limbs, making her muscles weak and her head swim. What she felt in Jessie's embrace was more than pleasure, more than passion. It was an unbearable hunger that threatened to undo her. She drank the sweetness of Jessie's mouth, quenching a thirst older than time.

"Jessie," Kate managed to say when she could bear to pull her mouth away from those sweet kisses, "what you make me feel. Oh my. Never...I *never* imagined."

So consumed with arousal she could not speak, Jessie buried her face in Kate's neck, breathless. Her stomach churned with the need to feel Kate's skin. She had no way to control what she had never expected, and she moaned helplessly with the ache of desire. She lifted trembling hands to Kate's face, finding those sweet lips once again, barely mindful of the ferocity of her caresses. Finally, kisses were not enough to assuage her need.

"Come lie with me, Kate?" Jessie dared ask, desperate for her.

Kate nodded wordlessly, trusting in the tenderness of Jessie's gaze.

Taking her hand, Jessie led Kate gently up the stairs to her bedroom. A large four-poster bed that had been her parents' occupied the center of the room on a broad braided rug. They stood close together, hands clasped, just inside the door, hesitating on the threshold of surrender.

"I love you, Kate," Jessie whispered, her voice breaking, an agony of desire shuddering through her frame. She wanted Kate so much that she was afraid to move.

Kate smiled, sensing every ripple of desire in Jessie's slender body and recognizing every flicker of longing in her face. Stepping away, she watched Jessie's expression as she slowly loosened the ties on her bodice. She slipped the dress from her shoulders, her pulse racing as she heard Jessie's quick intake of breath. Covered only by a light chemise, she returned to Jessie's

arms. Her nipples, taut under the thin material, brushed against
the rough denim of Jessie's shirt, and she gasped in surprise at
the jolt of excitement that coursed through her. Jessie's hands
were on her again, on her skin now. And everywhere Jessie
touched, Kate burned.

"I want to see you," Kate beseeched, her fingers working at
the buttons on Jessie's shirt.

Jessie stood motionless, a fine mist of sweat breaking out on
her face. Kate's breasts strained the cotton slip, shadows of pink
nipples, firm with anticipation, clearly visible. Jessie cupped
Kate's breasts in her palms, and Kate swayed against her, moaning softly. Jessie stilled, afraid that if she moved the great dam
inside her would burst, and she would do something to frighten
Kate. She ached to touch her, everywhere. Everywhere. Always.
Hesitantly, she rubbed her fingers over Kate's nipples.

Biting her lip, Kate struggled to see through a haze of
arousal. She finally loosened all the buttons on Jessie's shirt and
slid it off her shoulders. "Oh!" she cried when she saw the still
fresh scar on Jessie's chest. She pressed her lips to it, her hands
tenderly stroking Jessie's breasts.

Jessie groaned deep in her throat, lost. "Kate, oh Kate. I
can't bear it." When Kate's lips found her nipple in a soft kiss,
she broke at last. She picked Kate up in her arms and carried her
in a few quick strides to the bed. She leaned over her, naked
from the waist up, her arms braced on either side of Kate's body.
She kissed her again, on her mouth, on her neck, not gently this
time, but with a primal ferocity that had simmered unheeded for
far too long. Every kiss stoked her need. She reached for Kate's
chemise, the last barrier, and stopped herself. "Kate?" she
implored desperately, shivering with the ache in her depths.

Her hands fumbling with Jessie's heavy belt, Kate arched
her back. Her voice was unrecognizable to her own ears. "Hurry,
Jessie, please. I want to feel you against me."

Jessie swiftly kicked off her boots and stripped the levis
from her thighs. Kate removed the remaining obstacle between
them, and waited, naked and unafraid.

Jessie groaned as her gaze swept over Kate's body, taking in
her full firm breasts and the dark triangle of hair at the base of

her abdomen. She lay down upon her, carefully, guided by instinct. She found the places that made Kate sigh, first with her fingers and then, needing more, with her lips. She tasted her, drank her, devoured her, all the while thrilling to the soft sound of Kate's cries in her ears. When Kate arched from the bed, body taut and trembling, Jessie hesitated, afraid of her own desire.

"Jessie," Kate murmured, her eyes closed, her face flushed with arousal. She found Jessie's hand and drew those fingers to the heat between her legs, lifting her hips to allow Jessie inside. "Please."

Jessie almost whimpered as the hot slick folds surrounded her fingers. She rested her forehead on Kate's breast as she slowly, carefully entered her. Kate thrust against Jessie's palm, seemingly unaware of the small incoherent sounds escaping her throat. Jessie's chest constricted, her head throbbed, and a terrible pressure pounded through her limbs. She bit her lip and tried to hold onto reason.

Kate's eyes flew open in surprise. She grasped Jessie's shoulders convulsively, and pushed down hard, once, against Jessie's fingers. Then she was gone, shattering into a thousand separate moments of pleasure, trembling and crying Jessie's name.

As Kate clung to her, Jessie lost her fight for control. She brought her leg over Kate's, frantic for relief, and exploded at first contact. Her breath was wrenched from her as she spasmed. Then she collapsed, exhausted, into Kate's waiting arms.

⌘ ❖ ♦ ❖ ♦ ❖ ♦ ⌘

Kate awakened to the warm sun on her skin. It seemed to be late afternoon, and the air in Jessie's room was still and heavy. Her body felt languid and full from the effects of their loving, and she smiled to herself with the memory of their pleasure. She lay quietly, eyes closed, enjoying the weight of Jessie's hand on her breast.

Eventually, she opened her eyes and looked at Jessie, so innocent and vulnerable in sleep. Her fingers gently explored the line of Jessie's brow, the angle of her cheek, the soft curve of her lips. She raised herself so that she could see the length of Jessie's body, marveling at her loveliness. She lightly traced her fingers over the smooth column of Jessie's neck and along the edge of each delicate collarbone. Bending her head, she felt the softness of Jessie's breasts with her lips. Jessie stirred and moaned lightly in her sleep. Kate smiled. Tenderly, she curled her fingers in the blond hair between her lover's legs and kissed first her abdomen and then the pale skin where her thigh began.

Jessie's legs tensed, and she whispered hoarsely, "Kate...Kate, what are you doing?"

"Shhh, lie still. I'm loving you," she replied gently. She stroked the silk-soft flesh of Jessie's thighs, then higher, seeking the wet warmth she knew was there, teasing each delicate fold between her fingertips until Jessie moaned and shook. Emboldened by the urgent motion of Jessie's hips, she pressed her thumb to the stiff, engorged prominence and circled it, knowing Jessie as she knew herself. Unconsciously, she followed Jessie's body, matching her motions to Jessie's strangled cries. When Jessie arched, tight and trembling, Kate strummed her fingers hard and brought Jessie home.

Chapter
21

Jessie pulled the buckboard up behind the Schroeder house as the sun dropped low, a fading fireball almost ready to disappear behind the distant hills. She turned on the rough wooden seat to look at the young woman beside her. Her heart swelled with awe, the way it did when she stood, feeling small, before the majesty of the endless sky and the ageless land that sustained her. She was humbled at being entrusted with Kate's love, yet still stunned at the immense wonder of making love with her.

"I don't want to let you go," Jessie said softly. Kate's hand had rested on her thigh the entire hour it had taken her to drive into town, and Jessie didn't want her to move it. Ever. She questioned the rightness of being with Kate no more than she questioned the rightness of rising each morning to work her land. The places in her heart that had lain empty and waiting were filled. Her life seemed whole and all of a piece with Kate by her side. For her, it was simply the truth of things, and she thought no further than that. Loving Kate was right.

"I don't want to leave you either," Kate answered quietly. Of that she was certain. "I need to say hello to Hannah, so that my day won't be a lie, but I'll come back to the ranch as soon as I can get away again. My mother is starting to get used to me driving into town alone. She doesn't need to know I'm coming to you."

Kate's eyes were luminous, and her face flushed with more than the August heat. She couldn't think yet; her body was still too stirred. She had never experienced such an awakening of self, so suddenly, in both body and mind.

She had known, when barely in her teens, that she did not desire the future that was expected for her, but try as she might, she could not picture another. Certainly, she had heard of women who struck off on their own, many of them traveling into the western territories as teachers and seamstresses and laundresses. But Kate had not seen herself among them. She had not been raised to envision such independence and had only managed through her love of words and endless curiosity to discover that there were worlds beyond her own socially defined sphere. Still, nothing had ever prepared her for Jessie, or for what they had shared.

She knew little of what physical intimacies men and women enjoyed, having heard only veiled references from her mother and wild speculation from her girlfriends, but she knew what Jessie Forbes stirred in her. She knew what she held in her heart for this woman, and when that ardor echoed in her body, she welcomed it. Jessie's tenderness and answering passion fulfilled her. Why it was so, she could not say.

"I'll come to you again as soon as I can," Kate repeated firmly, needing to reassure herself as well as Jessie. She was already missing her.

"It will be a trial waiting," Jessie stated, her voice low, her fist opening and closing on her thigh as she struggled to describe her desire. She wanted Kate in her arms again; she wanted to hear Kate's cries of abandon as she touched her. She shuddered with the memory. "It's like I'm hungry for you, Kate."

"Jessie," Kate breathed, the wanting starting again. "I don't know what it is, but I can't stop thinking about being with you." She blushed. "Like we were today."

Jessie looked away, watching night approach as the blue sky flamed into purples, pinks, and deep oranges with the setting sun. She spoke quietly. "I don't have words for what happened, Kate. I don't know if there *are* words for it." She returned her gaze to Kate, her eyes burning brighter than the dazzling colors that surrounded them. Her body rippled with tension. "But I know that I love you. Life wouldn't mean much to me now without you. That won't ever change."

Kate smiled, her heart filling with the tenderness of Jessie's sweet, sure vows. "I love you, too."

For the moment, that seemed enough.

⌘ ❖ ◆ ❖ ◆ ❖ ◆ ⌘

Hannah rinsed out the dishtowel and hung it over the wooden rod inside her back door, watching the two women in the buckboard through her kitchen window. They were only talking, and she couldn't hear their words, but she didn't need to. She was watching their faces. Jessie had that solemn, serious expression on her face, the one Thaddeus had worn when he was working his way up to proposing, and Kate gazed at Jessie the way every young woman in love looks at her beau.

She wondered why she wasn't more surprised. She supposed it was because she had lived more than half her life on the frontier, and she had learned that city ways didn't count for much out here. There were women without husbands due to famine or fancy or fate, and they did what they had to do to get by. Some married for safety, forgoing love; some stepped up when widowed to fill their men's shoes, managing families and farms on their own; and some came west with no intention of being anybody's wife right from the start. Living close to the bone, with death a constant shadow, you learned fast to take what goodness life sent your way when you could, because sorrow was just over the horizon.

Looking at the two of them together, she couldn't see much harm to the caring. Sighing, she wondered what Martha might think if she was ever to be faced with it.

"Hannah," Kate said breathlessly as she came through the door, "I'm so sorry I'm so late. I met Jessie and—"

Hannah smiled, shushing her with a shake of her head. "That's fine, Kate. I like your company, and I'm always happy to see you, but you don't need to feel obliged to spend your time over here. I don't expect there's anything you'll need to know that you won't find out when the time comes."

Kate nodded, only half-listening as she watched Jessie untie her horse from the back of the buckboard and prepare to leave. Every movement of her graceful hands reminded Kate of the way they had felt on her body, and her head grew light with the memory. Jessie swung into the saddle, turned to the house, her eyes searching for Kate, and then she was gone with one last smile. Kate finally turned away from the window to find Hannah regarding her speculatively. Her face flamed because she was certain that Hannah could read every thought.

After pulling a tray of biscuits from the oven, Hannah slid the flat metal onto a cooling stone on the counter. "Jessie Forbes is a fine young woman. Works hard and turns an honest profit," she remarked, her back to Kate.

"Yes," Kate said cautiously.

Hannah wiped her hands on her apron as she turned to regard Kate steadily. "Next time you should invite her in for a drink before she has to ride all that dusty way back to her ranch."

Kate struggled for words and finally whispered, "Thank you, Hannah."

⌘ ❖ ◆ ❖ ◆ ❖ ◆ ⌘

"You're a sight for sore eyes, Montana," Mae said as she stepped up to the bar beside Jessie. "Seems I only see you any more when someone's plugged you full of holes."

"Hello, Mae." Jessie grinned sheepishly. "I was hoping you'd be around."

Mae studied her quizzically. "The sun's just set, Jess. The varmints won't be out for a while, so I'm not busy. Why don't you come sit a spell and tell me what brings you into town in the middle of the week?"

"How about you let me buy you dinner?" Jessie countered, wanting company. She had resisted going home because she knew the house would rattle with loneliness, and she already ached for Kate.

"I believe I'll take you up on that," Mae said, threading her arm through Jessie's. When they had moved into the dining room, she once again regarded her friend curiously. She didn't think she'd ever seen Jessie look moody before. "What're you fretting about, Montana?"

"Hmm? Oh. Why nothing, Mae," Jessie said quickly, blushing. She'd been thinking about waking up and feeling Kate's hands on her thighs, and about the way Kate knew just how to touch her in those spots that set her head to spinning, and how just when she didn't think she could stand another second without some part of her bursting, Kate had done just the right thing, and she *had* exploded. Remembering it brought the feelings back so strongly she almost gasped.

Mae leaned back in her chair, watching a flood of emotions play across the rancher's expressive features. How Jess ever managed to win at poker, she didn't know, because her face was an open book. And what Mae saw there made her heart sink. Jessie's eyes were a little hazy, and her skin was flushed under her tan. Her body almost quivered. Mae thought she could feel the heat radiating from her. Jessie Forbes looked like a woman who had been well loved, and recently.

She knew better than to ask, because Jessie was too honorable to tell. Instead, she casually asked, "What brings you in here today, Jess?"

"I drove Kate Beecher over to the Schroeder place," Jessie replied. She wanted to tell Mae about the extraordinary thing that had happened to her, but she barely had words for it herself. Plus, it was so intensely personal, so special, that she couldn't imagine sharing the details with anyone. "She was out my way, and it was getting late."

"Visiting, was she?" Mae probed.

Jessie smiled and nodded faintly. "Yes."

"How nice," Mae remarked coolly. She hoped that Kate knew what she was doing, because she was willing to bet that Jessie didn't. From the looks of her, she was too far gone already to see trouble coming.

"Well, Jess," Mae said softly, laying her hand on Jessie's arm. "You know you've always got a friend here if you ever need one."

Jessie looked at her quizzically, then took Mae's fingers lightly in hers. "I'll remember, Mae."

Chapter
22

Kate, her hair whipping behind her in the breeze, turned the buckboard expertly through the gates of the Rising Star ranch and looked expectantly toward the house. Her skin tingled with the familiar excitement that accompanied each visit. The sun had never felt so good, nor the air so clear. She pulled into the yard just as Jessie came out onto the porch. Kate drew a breath, seeing her again as if for the first time, only now her body held the memory of Jessie's caresses, and that alone was enough to stir her senses. She stepped onto the running board, her eyes dancing with happiness and the first awakening of desire as Jessie crossed the ground between them in quick eager strides.

"Kate!" Jessie cried, her hands on Kate's waist, swinging her down from the wagon exuberantly.

Kate laughed aloud and wrapped her arms around Jessie's neck, her lips searching for Jessie's as her feet touched the ground. They stood together under the bright morning sky, lost in their embrace, as carefree as they would ever be.

After a moment, Jessie pulled her head back, flushed and breathless. "Kate," she admonished teasingly, "I thought you wanted shooting lessons."

Kate knew from the way Jessie's hands strayed over her and the hoarse tone of her voice that Jessie's mind was not on the plans they had made either. Kate pressed her lips warmly against the tanned triangle of skin bared by Jessie's shirt and sighed contentedly.

"I did, until just a moment ago," she murmured, marveling at the way Jessie's touch aroused her. Even hours after she returned home, she still tingled where Jessie's hands and lips had stroked her. She had never imagined love would feel like this. That love would be a thing of the mind and the heart, yes. *But the wanting!* This was something so unexpected she could think of little else.

"We'd better go now, or I won't let you away for hours," Kate said reluctantly, but her tone was unconvincing. Even more telling was the rapid rise and fall of her chest as her breath grew short.

Jessie didn't let her go, but moved her lips close to Kate's ear instead. "We can always go later," she murmured, very aware of the trembling in her legs. "And I don't think I can ride now." She kissed the sweet skin of Kate's neck, and they both groaned. "I'm about to forget myself altogether."

Kate pushed her away, but her fingers brushed lightly over Jessie's breasts. "Inside the house," she whispered, watching Jessie's color rise and her pupils grow large. "Quickly."

They made it to the bottom of the staircase before Jessie grabbed Kate and pressed her to the wall, fingers searching for the ties on Kate's dress. Her hands were inside Kate's bodice an instant later, lifting her breasts free of their restraints.

"Lord, Kate," she groaned as she lowered her lips to Kate's hardening nipples, "I've missed you so."

Kate struggled to stand as a flood of arousal threatened to take her legs from under her. Her head fell back against the wall, and she curled her fingers in blond hair, pressing Jessie's face to her body. Jessie's tongue was on her, kindling a fire that spread downwards with unchecked abandon. It was always like this, and never the same. Jessie's desire inflamed her, and every ounce of her body responded. She quickened in a heartbeat and teetered on the brink of dissolving for long, agonizing, wonderful moments, crying Jessie's name, begging for her touch.

Sensing Kate's passion rising, Jessie became more insistent

with her caresses. Kate trembled against her, and there was a
desperate edge in her voice. With effort, Jessie raised her lips
from the sweet warmth of Kate's breast, gasping, "Wait, Kate.
Let me take you to bed."

Kate managed to open her eyes and shook her head, her
hands twisting in Jessie's shirt. Her eyes were huge dark pools of
yearning. "No," she choked. "No. Now. Now, please."

"Help me," Jessie demanded urgently, fired by Kate's need.
She lifted the light cotton dress for Kate to hold and knelt before
her. Gently, she pulled the final barriers aside and leaned forward, kissing the very center of Kate's desire. In response, Kate
jerked against her and cried out.

Jessie closed her eyes, her arms around Kate's hips, supporting her. She listened to her love while caressing her, tracing
the soft swell of engorged tissues with her tongue, sucking gently as Kate sobbed with pleasure. She followed the rhythm and
call of Kate's need, losing herself for long moments in the scent
and taste of her. Kate's hands fluttered over her face and through
her hair, leading her to the precious places she worshipped. She
felt Kate grow and harden under her tongue and knew without
telling that her release was near. She continued to stroke as Kate
arched against her mouth, feeling her own heart stop as the pulse
under her lips beat wildly.

She caught Kate as she was about to fall, standing quickly
and gathering her into her arms. Still inflamed by the same con-
suming heat, she kissed her love fiercely. Her breath tore from
her chest as she desperately pressed her hips forward.

"Kate," she groaned, barely able to see. "I...I need..." Her
voice trailed off into a strangled sob as she buried her face
against Kate's shoulder, shuddering.

"I know," Kate crooned, lightly caressing Jessie's fevered
face. "I know." She slipped her hand between them, squeezing
her palm to the soft material between Jessie's legs, cupping her.
She smiled as Jessie moaned. Quickly, she pulled each button
free, working her fingers under the material to find the warmth
waiting for her. As Kate squeezed the firm length of her, Jessie
swayed, weak with the pleasure of it. Kate met each thrust of her
love's hips with an answering pressure until Jessie stiffened and

cried out. When Jessie trembled in her arms, Kate laughed faintly, glorying in her.

⌘ ❖ ♦ ❖ ♦ ❖ ♦ ⌘

Jessie carried their picnic basket to the buckboard, Kate walking close beside her. Kate's fingers rested lightly on her arm. Jessie's body still tingled with the excitement they had just shared, and she couldn't stop grinning as she helped Kate up onto the seat.

"What?" Kate asked fondly, noting her satisfied expression.

"Just happy," Jessie answered, swinging up beside her. "Trying to figure out what I ever did to deserve you."

Kate moved her hand to Jessie's thigh, leaning against her as Jessie started the horses out of the yard. "You're just you," Kate said quietly, "and you don't ever have to do anything except love me."

Jessie glanced at her, suddenly serious. "I will, Kate. Always."

Kate snuggled closer, still languorous from their loving, and smiled contentedly. Jessie drove slowly through the lowlands and hills of her property, stopping frequently to point things out to the ever-curious young woman. The drive took in the summer grazing lands, sprinkled with wandering herds of horses, and the out cabins where she and the men stayed during branding times and roundups. From a hilltop overlooking impossibly green meadows, Jessie indicated the steeply rising mountains that bordered her land to the west.

"Those peaks are a natural protection for the highland meadows where the horses winter. When it starts to frost in the fall, we round up all the young and any pregnant mares and bring them down to that small canyon I showed you earlier. If the winter is really bad, they can't forage, and we feed them."

"Oh, Jessie," Kate exclaimed, awed by the scope of it all. "It's so beautiful. You must love it very much."

Jessie took Kate's hand and brought it to her lips. "I never thought I could love anything more. Until you."

Kate slipped her arm around Jessie's waist and rested her

head on the rancher's shoulder, stroking her arm through the soft cotton of her shirt. She thought how much she loved Jessie's simple strength and gentle heart. "Jessie," she murmured softly.

Jessie kissed her temple. "What?"

"I don't want things to ever change." Jessie was quiet so long that Kate leaned away to look at her face. "What's wrong?" she asked.

"I can't stand being apart from you so much, Kate," Jessie admitted at last, her voice low and tight. "I want us to lie down together at night and sleep side by side. I want to wake up with you." She looked at Kate, her eyes troubled. "I want...well, if I was a man, I'd want to marry you."

Kate's heart turned over. "Oh, Jessie," she breathed. "I love you."

Jessie searched Kate's face, finding all the courage she needed in that tender gaze. "I want you to come live with me, Kate. Will you?"

It was Kate's turn to be silent. When she spoke, her tone was anguished. "I want to. I want to be with you, married or not, for all my life." She stroked Jessie's cheek, her throat so tight she could barely speak. "But I don't know how."

"If you want to, Kate, that's all that matters to me right now. We'll figure it out," Jessie said, turning her head and kissing Kate's palm. "We've got time."

She climbed down and reached up for Kate. "Now, how about I give you that shooting lesson?"

Kate tried not to think of anything else as Jessie stood behind her, occasionally wrapping her arms around her to steady the Winchester, whispering encouragement in her ear. She even managed to hit the targets Jessie picked out now and then, but she couldn't quite rid herself of thoughts about confronting her parents. *How will I explain my desire to be with Jessie? How can I make them see that this is truly what I want for my life? And what will I do if they refuse?*

Chapter 23

Summer passed quickly, and the fall days were upon them before they knew it. Jessie's joy at returning home after hours on the range to unexpectedly find Kate quietly reading on the porch or preparing a meal in the kitchen was undiminished by the passage of time. Their love was simple and pure, and they grew closer as surely and naturally as two branches on the same tree, drawing nourishment from the same spring. The moments they spent together, talking and loving, were precious, bringing Jessie more happiness than she had dared dream of only a few months before. Still, she found herself wanting more.

There were days, sometimes even a week or more, between Kate's visits, and during those times, Jessie suffered from more than loneliness. She couldn't help but think of Ken Turner, who she knew still paid court to Kate. It tormented her to think that he might touch Kate, when *she* could not even arrive unannounced at her door, asking only for the pleasure of sitting by her side.

Each time she walked Kate to the buckboard and watched her drive away or rode with her to the edge of town, it was harder to let her go. The nights when she lay down alone were colder and longer than any she could ever recall. She was lonely in a way she never had been before, because now there were places in her heart that only Kate could fill.

"Kate?" Jessie asked late one afternoon, lying naked with Kate in her arms under a heavy quilt. A fire burned in the hearth in the bedroom. Kate's back was to her front, and she buried her face in Kate's thick hair, smoothing her hands slowly over Kate's stomach until she cupped her breasts in her hands.

Kate stilled Jessie's movement, pressing her palms over Jessie's hands. "I can't think when you do that," Kate admonished lightly, but there was no disapproval in her tone. She loved Jessie's hands on her. "What is it?"

Closing her eyes, Jessie sighed, trying to shut out every sensation but Kate. She couldn't, as much as she wished to. "Winter comes early out here, Kate. It will snow soon."

"Yes," Kate said quietly, her grip on Jessie's hands tightening. She waited.

"It's not safe for you to come here any longer," Jessie continued, each word feeling like it was tearing a piece of her heart as she spoke it. "You could be caught in a blizzard and freeze to death quicker than a minute."

"I can't stay away," Kate whispered. "I can't be without you." She couldn't imagine a week, let alone the long months of winter, separated from her love.

Jessie tightened her arms around her, pulling Kate even closer. "I can't have anything happening to you, Kate," she murmured. "I'm not made strong enough for that. Promise me you won't drive out here alone again."

Kate nodded. She knew Jessie was right, and she would never worry her, even though it would be devastating to go all winter without seeing her. She turned within the circle of Jessie's arms, searching her face, seeing the misery in her eyes. "We must find another way." She sought Jessie's mouth, kissing her lightly at first, then with a sudden hunger. She drew away with a small cry. "I *won't* be without you."

"I'll come into town when I can," Jessie ventured. "Maybe you could come to the hotel?" Even as she said it, she knew that it was impossible. The weather was unpredictable at best in the foothills of the Rockies, and even if she could leave the ranch, how would she get a message to Kate to let her know that she had come? And meeting at the hotel? Impossible. There was no way that they could ever keep that fact from Kate's parents for long. Plus, part of her resisted the idea of meeting Kate for an afternoon's passion, as if that were all there was between them. She never tired of feeling Kate close to her or of loving her for hours on end, but she took just as much joy in raising her eyes from some bit of work to find Kate sitting nearby with a book in her hands.

"I must speak to my parents," Kate said quietly, knowing the time had come. She could not go on indefinitely avoiding Ken Turner's persistent demands, nor could she pretend to her parents that her reluctance was only because she was not certain that she wished to be *his* wife. Having lain with Jessie, she could never be any man's wife. Jessie was her heart. "I'll make them understand."

"I'll come with you," Jessie said firmly, moving to get up. "They'll never need worry for your safety nor your care, not as long as I live, nor after either. I owe them the comfort of knowing that."

"Wait," Kate cried, holding her fast. "We have time before I need to be back." She stretched out in Jessie's arms, her legs entwining naturally with those of her taller lover. "I'll not let go of you yet."

Jessie smiled, turning them so Kate lay beneath her, and lowered herself gently upon her. Her chest filled with an almost unbearable sensation of tenderness and wonder, and she set about showing Kate just how much she cherished her. With her lips, with her mouth, with her work roughened hands turned to velvet on Kate's sweet skin, she told her. Her kisses carried the promises, and her touch conveyed the certainty that she so often had no words to express. *I will love you,* Jessie's caresses vowed, *with all my being, for all my life. You are my reason and my answer and my purpose,* her fingers pledged, each knowing stroke carrying Kate closer to fulfillment.

"I love you, Kate, I love you," she finally whispered, her face pressed to Kate's neck. An inarticulate moan escaped Kate's throat, as she arched under Jessie's ministrations.

Jessie held her love until she quieted and caressed her

lightly while she dozed. The rancher could not remember what
her existence had been like before Kate, and she could not imagine a life without her now.

⌘ ❖ ◆ ❖ ◆ ❖ ◆ ⌘

"I want to come with you," Jessie said again, stubbornly
insistent.

They sat just up the road from Kate's house; Star was tied to
the back of the buckboard, waiting patiently. Darkness was falling, and the night was cold. Kate sat wrapped in a heavy wool
blanket, her cloak fastened tightly around her. Jessie wore a
heavy sheepskin coat, with her hat pulled low, her hands bare.
Their breath hung in the air, a reminder that they had very little
time before nature made separation inevitable.

Kate slipped her fingers from her glove and took Jessie's
hand. It was warm. "I know you do, Jessie. But let me talk with
them first." Her head ached just thinking about what her mother
was going to say.

"They need to know what I feel for you," Jessie persisted. It
was only proper that she speak up. "I don't want you to do this
alone, Kate. It's not right."

Kate looked at her quickly, hearing a note of worry in her
tone. "You don't think that I'll let them talk me out of it, do
you?" Jessie turned to her, and the surprise in her eyes reassured
Kate.

"No, never," Jessie stated firmly. "That's not what I was
thinking. I don't suppose there's a word for what we are to each
other, but I know that you are the only one I'll ever love. I want
us to be together, and the closest word I know to that is married."

"Yes, I want that, too," Kate responded, her shoulders set
with resolve. "You go have dinner at the hotel and then come
back to the house around eight o'clock. We can all talk then."

"Oh, Kate, I can't eat," Jessie protested. "My stomach feels
like a nest of rattlers."

Kate felt dizzy with apprehension, too. "Then go to the bar
and talk to Frank."

Jessie didn't like it, but they were Kate's parents, and she supposed it made some sense to get them used to the idea before she showed up on their doorstep. She bit back a further protest as she helped Kate down from the wagon. Kate swayed suddenly, and Jessie gripped her tightly.

"What's wrong?" she asked, alarmed at Kate's pallor.

Kate smiled tremulously, oddly breathless. She shook her head, answering, "It's nothing. I'm just nervous." She reached a hand to brush Jessie's cheek. "I'm fine. You go on now. I'll see you in a little while."

Watching Kate walk away from her, Jessie stood by the side of the buckboard, a sinking feeling in her chest. She felt helpless and unexpectedly very much afraid.

⌘ ❖ ♦ ❖ ♦ ❖ ♦ ⌘

"Something wrong with Frank's whiskey?" Mae asked. "You been standing there with that same drink in front of you for better than an hour."

Jessie looked up, a vacant expression in her eyes. She stared at Mae a second, then smiled weakly. "No. His whiskey's fine."

Mae peered at her, surprised by the bleak tone of her voice. "What's happened? You look like a whipped dog."

"I feel like one," Jessie said bitterly. "Probably worse."

Mae motioned to Frank for a bottle. "Bring your glass, and let's sit for a minute, Jess. You'd best tell me what's going on."

They took a table in the far corner of the saloon, and Jessie told her. She stared at the glass cupped between her fingers, her head down, her voice unsteady, as she spoke of Kate, and their love, and their plans. When she reached the part where she had gone back to the Beecher house that evening, she finally raised her eyes and met Mae's.

"Her father came to the door and stepped out onto the porch when he saw that it was me," Jessie said hollowly. "He told me, very politely, that Kate was indisposed and could not see me. He also said that he thought it best that I not come around again, seeing that Kate would be very busy soon preparing for her wedding to Mr. Turner."

She downed the shot, then held out an unsteady hand for the

bottle, pouring another. "He never even raised his voice, but the look on his face could have frozen a pond in the middle of summer." She emptied the glass and set it down hard. "I'd rather he'd've hit me."

Mae stared at her, trying to absorb the tale. As she listened, her emotions had run the gamut from despair to faint hope. Her initial reaction had been shock. She hadn't known what to expect after Kate's visit, but it hadn't been this. Hearing Jessie tell it, watching her face, Mae could see how much Jess loved the girl, and it almost broke her heart. Then, when she heard that Kate's father had put a stop to the relationship, her response had been relief and, *God help me*, happiness.

"Maybe it's for the best, Jess," she said gently. *You'll get over her; she's not right for you,* she wanted to scream. But part of her didn't believe it, as much as she wanted to. She remembered the blaze in Kate's eyes when she had said that she loved Jessie, and she heard the torment in Jessie's voice now. They loved each other all right.

Jessie's eyes were wounded as she met Mae's gaze. "How?" she asked brokenly. "How could it be for the best? I love her, and she loves me."

"Her parents would never accept it," Mae continued softly. "A girl like her is supposed to be married. They won't know no other way."

Jessie swallowed. "What about what *she* wants? What about Kate's happiness?"

Mae couldn't help but laugh, but there was no humor in her voice. "Lord's sake, Jess. Whenever did the feelings of a woman matter in these things?"

"Kate matters, Mae," Jessie said firmly, a spark of life returning to her eyes. "She matters to me more than anything in this world."

"More than the ranch?" Mae asked, wanting to show Jessie the hopelessness of her dream. "Because if you think they're just gonna let her move on out there with you, without a fight, you're more drunk than two whiskeys would make you."

Jessie was quiet a long time, thinking about the look on Martin Beecher's face. She knew when a man couldn't be swayed. "No, I suppose they wouldn't."

"Don't do anything foolish, Montana," Mae said as tenderly as she could. She saw a cowboy approaching from the corner of her eye and cursed under her breath. "Some things aren't meant to be, even if they seem right," she cautioned as she rose to greet the stranger.

Jessie watched Mae walk away with the cowboy, sad to see her go. She sat for a long time, turning the empty glass on the scarred tabletop, until she knew what she must do.

Chapter
24

Kate approached the Schroeder's back door the next morning burdened in body and soul, an overwhelming sense of hopelessness leaving her dazed. She had barely slept, her head ached horribly, and she hadn't been able to manage more than a bit of juice at breakfast. Though she had no idea how she would get through a morning with Hannah without crying, the thought of staying at home to face her mother's silent admonitions was even more daunting. As she slowly climbed the stairs to the back porch, Kate was surprised to see Hannah Schroeder emerging in a rush, her expression expectant, as if she had been waiting for Kate to arrive.

"Come inside, Kate," she said kindly, holding the door for her. "It's freezing out here."

Kate nodded absently, but she was having trouble putting one foot in front of the other. Everything seemed so impossible. Faced with the harsh reality of her utter powerlessness to go against her parents' wishes, she felt like a prisoner in her own life. *I am a prisoner—of convention and custom and the narrow-minded views of the very people who say they love me. They wouldn't even* listen *to me—how can that be love?*

"Come stand by the stove. You're shaking," Hannah directed as she took Kate's arm, guiding her into the kitchen.

"Thank you," Kate said hoarsely. Her throat was dry, almost parched. The heat from the ovens accosted her, and, for an instant, she felt dizzy. She swayed slightly, and Hannah slipped a protective arm around her waist to steady her. Kate loosened her scarf with trembling hands and slipped out of her cloak.

Looking at her charge with a worried frown, Hannah passed a cool hand over Kate's forehead. "You look peaked. You'd best take care. Sally down at the dry goods store says there's quite a few people down with the grippe."

Kate shook her head. "I'm fine." She gave a tremulous smile, but her eyes brimmed with tears.

"Well," Hannah said quietly, "you've got a visitor. Go on in the parlor there. I'll bring you some biscuits and tea. You look like you could use something."

Confused, Kate stared at her. "A visitor?"

"Go on, now," Hannah urged gently.

Kate passed through the quiet house toward the room at the end of the hall where she had met the Schroeders on her very first morning in New Hope. She had been a different woman then, bright and eager and filled with expectations. All she could imagine now was a dark future that held no hope of liberty or love. She stepped into the room and stared at the familiar figure waiting by the window. She closed her eyes briefly, sure that she was dreaming.

"Jessie?" she whispered when she could speak.

"Kate."

And then Jessie's arms were around her, and Kate was clinging to her, sobbing with a combination of joy and piercing sorrow. *Will this be the last time I hold you? Oh, my love...* She pressed her cheek to Jessie's shoulder, silently seeking shelter in her lover's embrace.

"My Kate," Jessie murmured into her hair, stroking her tenderly. "It's all right. It's all right."

But Kate knew that it would never be all right again. "Oh, Jessie. I was afraid when my father wouldn't let me speak to you last night that I might never see you again. But you didn't leave me."

"No, never," Jessie assured her swiftly, her heart thudding

painfully at the thought. Feigning a confidence she didn't feel, she went on as steadily as she could. "What did they say to you? Tell me what happened, love."

Her mind still numb, Kate spoke slowly. "My parents think I've become unbalanced. That the move out here from Boston has done things to me." She laughed harshly, a sob forming at the end. "Mother is sure that I've had some kind of breakdown, and Father thinks that being uprooted from home has caused me to suffer a lapse in judgment."

Jessie shook her head, trying to make sense of Kate's halting story. "Because you love me?"

Kate smiled, her first real smile. Jessie's steadfast presence settled her nerves, and she felt sanity returning after the nightmare of the previous evening. *This, this woman, this love, is real.*

When she spoke again, her voice was calmer. "No, my darling. Because I *don't* love Ken Turner." At Jessie's continued look of confusion, Kate went on, "My mother actually tried to be somewhat understanding. She allowed that women often form close affections, particularly during stressful times, but every woman knows that those friendships must take a second seat to the responsibilities of a wife. She thinks that I simply need to see that."

Trying to make sense of this as she listened, Jessie grew still. "They think that if you marry him you won't love me any more?"

"No," Kate said quietly. "As long as I don't see you and perform my wifely duties as expected with Ken, I don't think it matters at all to them if I love you or not. We will just not speak of it." She recalled the dark look in her father's eyes as he had pronounced that she would accept Ken Turner's proposal, which she should have done months ago, and that they would hear no more of her foolish desire to live at the Rising Star ranch with Jessie Forbes.

Jessie's jaw clenched. "Can they force you to marry him?"

"No," Kate replied. "They love me, despite how it looks. If I refuse, they won't disown me."

"Well," Jessie sighed, grasping at any small glimmer of

hope, "that's something. Maybe if we give them a little time and
then talk to them again—together—we can make them understand."

Her own eyes dark with anguish, Kate gazed into Jessie's
face. She traced the strong line of Jessie's jaw with trembling
fingers, aching with love for her and knowing how much she was
about to hurt her. "They won't put me out on the street, but my
father was quite clear about the consequences if I don't do as
they say. They'll send me back to Boston as soon as the roads are
passable in the spring if I fail to marry by then. There's no way I
can imagine to change their minds." Her heart nearly broke as
she watched the color drain slowly from Jessie's face and her
expression collapse with pain. Watching tears form in her lover's
eyes was worse than any agony she could suffer herself. "I'm so
sorry, Jessie. I'm so sorry."

"Oh, Lord," Jessie whispered, terror finally making her
shake. "They can't send you away." She gripped Kate's shoulders in a tortured grasp, her eyes wild. "Can they, Kate?"

"I *am* of age," Kate said slowly, "but how can I defy them? I
have neither funds of my own nor any real means of supporting
myself. And where could I go?"

Jessie's temper flared, although her anger was not at Kate.
"You can come to me. I *love* you, Kate. You belong with me."
Jessie made an effort to control herself. Searching Kate's eyes,
she asked, "That's what you want, isn't it? That would make you
happy?"

"Oh, Jessie. Yes!" Kate kissed her quickly. "You make me
happier than I've ever been. You're the only thing that matters to
me. You must know I love you with all my heart."

"Then come be with me," Jessie implored. Her voice broke,
her throat tightening with love and fear and hope. "Please."

Kate stroked Jessie's arm tenderly. "Oh my love, if only I
could. But my father would never allow it. He would know that I
had gone to you, and he would look for me there. I'm not sure
what he would do, but I won't have you hurt by this."

"Hurt?" Jessie cried, her body stiff with rage. "Hurt? What
will I do if they take you from me? How do you think I could
live after that? I'd have nothing without you."

Kate slipped her arms around Jessie's waist, holding her as if never to let her go. "Nor I, without you."

Moments passed as they stood together, struggling for calm and reason in a world suddenly gone mad. At last Jessie spoke, her voice quiet and resigned. "Then we have to leave here. We'll go away, further west to the Oregon territory. There's gold there still." She drew another deep breath, her resolve growing. "I can even pass for a man if there's need. It's happened before without my meaning it."

Kate drew a sharp breath. "No! You can't leave the Rising Star. It's your home."

The determined young rancher held Kate at arm's length and looked deeply into her eyes. "There would be no home for me anywhere without you, Kate. I will not let you go."

Kate saw the certainty in Jessie's blue eyes, and something she needed to see even more—the love. "Oh, Jessie, I'm so sorry about your ranch."

Smiling tenderly, Jessie shook her head. "It's all right, love. Who knows, maybe we'll be able to come back after a season or two." She refused to consider what it would be like to leave the Rising Star. She knew what it was like there without Kate, and there was no choice at all as to what needed to be done. "We'll need to leave very soon, before the mountain passes are snowed in."

Kate stepped away and drew a deep breath, feeling suddenly stronger. "When?"

"Before the end of the week."

"Yes," she said, thinking also that they had no choice. An instant later she smiled, a firm resolute smile, realizing that for the first time in her life she *did* have a choice, and her choice was Jessie.

"When can you be ready to leave?" Jessie asked quietly.

"Soon," Kate said purposefully. "There are only a few things that I want to bring, but I must gather them without my parents' notice. The day after tomorrow?"

Jessie nodded, already planning what she needed to buy on her way out of town. Everything else she had at the ranch. She'd settle at the bank and talk to Jed. She could trust him. "We'll leave in two days then."

Kate flung herself into Jessie's arms. "Oh my love, I'm so sorry."

Jessie held her to her breast. "Don't be, Kate. Your love is all that matters to me."

⌘ ❖ ◆ ❖ ◆ ❖ ◆ ⌘

Hannah watched Jessie ride out of the yard. She turned as Kate came quietly into the kitchen.

"I need to go home, Hannah," Kate said softly. "I'm sorry I can't stay."

"No need to worry," Hannah said, packing some hot biscuits into a basket along with a jar of jam. "Take these. You'll be hungry sooner or later."

Kate smiled fondly. "You've been very kind. I don't know how my mother or I would have managed without all your help. Thank you."

The older woman looked at Kate steadily, noting the tear stains still damp on her cheeks and the hint of misery in her eyes. It wasn't any of her affair, but it was plain to see that the child was suffering. Seemed to her that Jessie Forbes had looked the same when she had come to the back door just after sun-up, asking if she might wait for Kate. Didn't take much sense to see that something serious had happened, and she had a feeling she knew what it was. If it was Martin and Martha coming between those two, she didn't see any hope for them. She knew what Kate's folks wanted for their daughter's future, and these young girls weren't going to be able to change those ideas.

She sighed and handed Kate her cloak. "Sometimes those that love us cause more hurt with the loving than they do with anger. You have to be forgiving, if you can."

Kate kissed Hannah lightly on the cheek and nodded, knowing that she had already forgiven her parents. She wished she could have had their understanding, but there was no time left to wait. She was not leaving to spite them, merely to save herself. As she hurried home in the cold morning air, she turned her mind to the future, and, finally, hope returned to her heart.

Chapter
25

Kate's head ached terribly and the house seemed intolerably warm as she hurried about gathering up the few clothes and personal treasures that she could not leave behind. Her father was at the newspaper office, and her mother was out running errands. It was the first chance that she had had to pack.

She had written a letter to her parents explaining what she had done, praying with each painful sentence that they would understand and someday believe that she was happy. She had put the envelope on her bedside table, intending to leave it in the kitchen the next day for them to find. She wanted to get everything ready so that she could leave as soon as the house was empty in the morning.

Tomorrow was Martha's day to visit her new friends at the ladies' weekly luncheon gathering. *Tomorrow*, she thought, *tomorrow I will go to Jessie, and we will make a new life.*

It had only been twenty-four hours since they had parted, but she already missed Jessie terribly. Now, when things were so very hard, she needed her near. Jessie was always so calm, so steady. So strong.

When she thought of her leaving her beloved ranch, Kate's heart ached. She had only to envision her standing on the wide front porch looking contentedly out over her land, or astride one

of her great horses, grinning and confidant and so totally at'
peace, to know what a great sacrifice Jessie was making. Kate
hated for her to give up such a part of herself, but she could not
imagine any other way. They could not stay, and Kate could not
give her up. *If I lost Jessie, it would surely kill me. We must go.*

Upstairs in her room, Kate opened her travel trunk, the one
she had packed with such optimism less than a year before. She
passed a trembling hand over her forehead, wiping with a handkerchief at the icy sweat that had broken out there. Then she felt
suddenly cold. Shivering, she reached for a shawl. As she finished filling the suitcase, adding her slim book of sonnets to rest
on top, she remembered sitting by Jessie's bedside reading them.
The thought of Jessie warmed her even as her body grew more
chilled.

She dragged the heavy valise toward her closet, suddenly
feeling lightheaded. Remembering that she had had no breakfast,
being much too nervous to eat, she could not recall now if she
had even eaten dinner the night before. As the room started to
tilt, she grasped the dresser for support. It was becoming more
difficult by the moment to think clearly.

"I must get something to drink," she murmured, frightened
by the trembling in her limbs. She descended the staircase
unsteadily and made her way carefully to the kitchen. With one
hand trailing along the wall, she struggled to stay upright. She
found a pitcher of tea her mother had left in the heavy icebox
and carried it with shaking hands to the table. *A bit of bread and
honey is all I need.* Her vision wavering slightly, she laid the
shawl aside, much too warm now.

As she reached for a glass, her head spun and a wave of nau-
sea overtook her. She clutched the counter, her knees buckling,
the room swirling about her. A curtain of gray obscured her
vision, and she was dimly aware of the cool kitchen floor under
her cheek. Barely conscious, too weak to rise, she called Jessie's
name.

In short order, she lost all sense of time. At some point
though, she was aware of being moved and of voices rising and
falling somewhere far away. She struggled weakly, protesting
incoherently, as someone removed her clothing. She tried des-

perately to focus, knowing there was something she must do. Somewhere she must go. Eventually, her body surrendered to the fever, and she slipped into total unconsciousness with Jessie's name, now unspoken, on her lips.

⌘ ❖ ♦ ❖ ♦ ❖ ♦ ⌘

Jessie paced the length of the porch, watching the dusk give way to darkness. A tarp-covered wagon stood waiting behind the house, packed with all they would need for their trip over the Rockies. Star and Rory were fed and bridled, ready for the journey as well. She stood at the rail, one arm braced along the porch post, staring toward the cookhouse. There were lights in the windows and the smell of stew in the air. Jed would be there, with the men. *God, it's hard, saying goodbye.*

Jed had said little when she told him she was leaving. He had stood quietly, chewing thoughtfully on a piece of hay, as Jessie explained that she would send legal papers giving him the authority to handle all the business affairs of the ranch. She thought at one point her voice would give out, but she held steady and looked him in the eye while she talked.

When she finished and fell silent, Jed had looked past her toward the mountains, as if gauging the climb. "You'll need to hurry if you're going to beat the snows," he said finally.

"Yes," she replied, waiting.

He had taken off his hat and brushed it lightly against his thigh. They were leaning against the corral fence, the two of them, hunched in their heavy jackets, eyes tearing faintly in the cold wind. "I know you ain't running from the law," he said at length.

"No."

"There are only two things I know that will make a man leave his home," Jed remarked quietly, his eyes still fixed on the distant hills. "The law or a woman."

She stiffened slightly, pushed her hands a little deeper in the pockets of her jacket. "Yes."

He looked back at her, and all he saw was the same clear gaze and steady strength he had always seen. "Ain't nothing you can do but leave?"

Her eyes grew dark with pain, the anger gone now. "No."

"Well," he said after another long pause. "When you feel you can come back, it will all still be here waitin'. I can assure you that."

They had remained a while longer, their shoulders barely touching, watching the sky cloud over and the wind blow bare branches around the yard. She was glad for his company because it kept the sadness away.

That had been hours ago, and Kate should have arrived before sundown. Jessie looked up the road in the descending gloom for the hundredth time, even though she knew in her heart that Kate would have come by now if she were coming at all. Something must have happened. Perhaps she had been discovered.

A faint voice in the back of her mind kept whispering that perhaps Kate had thought better about leaving and changed her mind—that she would have come had she wanted to. Perhaps at the final moment, she could not say goodbye. Too much risk, too much loss. Jessie could almost understand if that's what had happened. It would be harder for Kate than for her, leaving everything behind. Maybe what they shared wasn't enough, maybe...maybe...

"No," she growled under her breath, pacing again. *I can't believe it.* She truly couldn't. She remembered Kate's eyes when she had declared that she loved her. She remembered Kate's touch, and her smile, and her soft sighs as they lay quietly wrapped in one another after loving. Of course Kate would come. She had said that she would. But the night said otherwise.

As total darkness finally surrounded her, Jessie sat on the steps, weary from the hours of anxious waiting, elbows propped on her knees, her head down. She stared bleakly at nothing, her mind a blank. The star-filled sky revolved slowly overhead, and the night air drew down around her, but she remained motionless, impervious to the cold that slowly chilled her to the bone.

When all the lights were out in the bunkhouses, and even the night seemed to sleep, she roused herself. Star and Rory still waited patiently, tied to the wagon, and she could not leave them unsheltered in the brutal wind. Mechanically, she walked them down to the barn, removed their bridles, and led them into stalls. Then she made her way back up to the house, pausing on the porch to search the dark with desperate eyes, hoping to see deliverance emerge from the shadows. She swayed slightly, grasping the banister to steady herself, running a hand over her face, surprised at the moisture on her cheeks. She couldn't feel anything, not even the tears. Then, very slowly, she turned her back to the road, walked into the house, and shut the door behind her.

Chapter
26

For four days, the illness had raged through New Hope, and with each passing day, the panic seizing the townspeople grew. Almost half the families in town had been struck by the fast-moving influenza, and everyone had a friend or loved-one sick with the high fevers, wracking coughs, and suffocating bloody fluids in the lungs. In some homes, there had been deaths, mostly among the very young or the very old, the ones with little strength to fight the rampaging infection. But here and there, it was a young man or woman, struck down suddenly, and taken within hours. Those who had escaped the disease were afraid to leave their homes, and the streets lay eerily deserted. The few who were too restless or too stubborn to stay inside congregated at the saloon.

Frank had come down sick the previous day, and Mae and those of her girls who were still well were looking after the customers in the bar. Conversation was slight, most men lingering remorsefully over half-finished drinks, not wanting to talk of news that seemed all bad. Mae tried to keep up appearances, chatting briefly with each newcomer, forcing a smile. She stared in surprise at the newest face in the long row of unshaven men leaning against the bar. Thaddeus Schroeder nodded hello, his face drawn and pale.

"Thaddeus," Mae said warmly, "never expected to see you in here during daylight hours. Wish it was under better circumstances. What can I get you?"

Thaddeus smiled wanly. "A good strong whiskey, Mae. Things are getting terrible, just terrible."

Mae looked at him pityingly and poured him a drink. "How are your people, Thaddeus?" she asked gently.

He looked at her with sorrowful eyes. "My John Emory's ailing with it, but Doc said last night that the boy had passed the crisis, thank the good Lord. He wasn't sick at all just three days ago, and then..." His voice broke and he looked away. "So fast. It comes so fast." He cleared his throat and reached for the glass that Mae had filled for him. "Doc says we're probably lucky to have lived through that terrible spell in '52. Makes us stronger now, he says."

She patted his hand. "That's fine, Thaddeus, just fine."

Mae had missed the terrible epidemic that swept over the western plains and beyond, over a decade before, decimating the Indian populations and new settlers as well. But she had seen the effects of the devastating infection in the crowded tenements of New York City, and death looked the same everywhere. She prayed that this outbreak would be over quickly and the losses few. Lord, life was hard enough without this, too.

But Thaddeus was beyond consoling. He had come to the saloon because he needed to talk, and he couldn't burden his wife, who was so busy herself looking after the boy and helping the neighbors, too. He continued to ramble, almost to himself. "There are so many, Mae. So many others sick with it." He sighed. "More will die, God help us."

"Thaddeus," Mae said kindly, touching his hand again. "These people are strong, pioneer stock. They'll survive. Don't you be giving up hope now."

He raised remorseful eyes to hers. "It's Martin and Martha Beecher I feel so bad about. They're not like the rest of us, not used to such hardships. I feel like it's my fault for bringing them out here. That girl is going to be on my conscience, Mae." Tears brimmed in his eyes, and he reached quickly for his handkerchief.

Mae stared at him, an awful fear crowding out her breath. "Thaddeus, what are you talking about?"

"It's their daughter, Kate," he replied when he managed to contain himself. "She came down with the illness yesterday, and Doc says she's very bad. Might not even make it 'til tomorrow." He finished his drink. "My fault. All my fault."

Mae wanted to scream at him to hush so she could think. *Kate dying? That couldn't be, could it? Not young, beautiful, vibrant Kate. But of course it could.* There was no rhyme or reason to these things, and very little one could do to change fate. Not a thing, really.

She turned away from the lonely man, unable to summon any words of solace. She moved sadly down the bar, pouring shots of inadequate comfort for the mourners.

⌘ ❖ ◆ ❖ ◆ ❖ ◆ ⌘

The house had a dark, deserted look about it. The windows were dead eyes staring back at her, and not even a breath of smoke curled from the chimney. For an instant, her heart seized with terror. What if death had visited here already? Would anyone have thought to tell her? Wouldn't she have known somehow if Jess were gone? Controlling her panic, Mae knocked on the wide front door. When there was no answer, she pushed open the door and hesitantly stepped inside. It was cold, as if all life had indeed departed days before.

"Who is it?" a low, quiet voice said out of the darkness.

Startled, Mae cried out sharply, her eyes searching the hallway, trying to peer into the room in the direction of the voice. "Jess? For God's sake, Jess, is that you?"

Suddenly a match flared, flickered, and then caught. A moment later lamplight illuminated the library in a faint yellow glow. Jessie stood wraith-like by the fireplace, pale and hollow-eyed. She placed the lamp on the mantle and turned slowly toward Mae, her normally straight back slumped, her gaze dazed and listless.

"What is it, Mae?" she asked slowly. She gripped the edge of the stone ledge tightly, a little unsteady on her feet. She hadn't had much to eat. Couldn't remember her last meal actually. The fireplace was empty; she hadn't cooked. She dimly recalled Jed coming up to the house that morning, or maybe it was the night before, asking after her. He was saying he had seen the wagon still out back, warning that the snows were coming any day. She had sent him away, telling him she wouldn't be needing the wagon after all. He had wanted to say more, she could see the worry in his face, but she had shut the door. There was nothing to say.

Jessie looked up from the cold hearth, surprised to see Mae still standing there, staring at her. She cleared her throat. "What is it?" she asked again.

Mae came forward slowly, wondering if Jessie was sick with what everyone else had. She looked so drained, so empty. Mae had never seen her look like this, not even right after her father had been killed. "Jess," she said quietly. "Jess, are you sick?"

"No," Jessie said with a shake of her head, confused. She didn't feel anything. That strange numbness was still there, everywhere. She guessed it always would be.

"Then what are you doing in here in the dark?" Mae was so worried and so scared she was beginning to lose her temper. "It's freezing in here, too! Are you *trying* to get sick?"

The hard edge in Mae's voice penetrated Jessie's muddled consciousness. "I'm not sick," she said, a little of the life returning to her voice. "What are you talking about? Why do you keep asking that? Why are you here?"

Mae gasped. "Lord, you don't know, do you?"

"Know what?" Jessie asked, an ominous dread stirring in her chest. "What's happening?"

"The grippe," Mae said bitterly. "It hit town a bit ago, and the last two days have seen some sorrow."

Slowly, Jessie's face lost its last trace of color. "Kate," she whispered. *God, I am such a fool! Why didn't I go into town and look for her? How could I let my doubts keep me away?* She grabbed Mae's shoulders, leaning down to look into her face. Her eyes were wide and wild. "Kate! Is she sick?"

Mae paused, not sure until just that moment what she had come to say. The torment and terror in Jessie's face convinced her. She nodded, then said very quietly, "She's bad, Jess. Doc says she doesn't have long."

Jessie's head snapped back as if she had been struck. For a moment, she was completely still, the only movement a faint pulse beating in her neck. Then a horrible glint flashed in her eyes and a sound more like a snarl than a word tore from her throat.

"No!"

Mae reached for her as Jessie snatched her gunbelt from the table and strapped it on. "Jess," she said hesitantly, afraid of what Jessie might do in her state of mind. "Her family—"

The look Jessie gave her stopped Mae cold.

"There's not a man alive can keep me from her, Mae," Jessie answered stonily, heading for the door. "I can't let her die without me there."

Chapter
27

A commotion at the front door roused Martha from an uneasy slumber. She had been restlessly napping in the small sitting room adjoining Kate's bedroom while Hannah kept watch. Martin had retired to his library hours before, too distraught to sit vigil at his daughter's bedside. Hannah came into the room just as Martha was rising.

"Whoever is at the door?" Martha asked impatiently. "They'll disturb Kate."

Hannah regarded Martha sympathetically, not mentioning that Kate had not been aware of anything for some time. Martha's hair was falling from its pins, her eyes were hollow, and her face gaunt. *Poor woman*, Hannah thought, and whispered a quick prayer of thanks that her own son was on the mend. "It's Jessie Forbes. Martin is talking with her now."

Martha stared uncomprehendingly for a moment, her confused expression quickly turning to alarm. "Here? She's here?"

Hannah nodded. She and Martha had had no chance to talk about any of the events of the last few days. She had only just that evening been able to leave John Emory and had come straight to the Beecher house, knowing that Martha would need help looking after Kate. As soon as she arrived, she sent Martha off for some much needed rest.

She had been sitting by Kate's bedside, sponging the fever sweat from her face and neck when she first heard the pounding on the front door. Afraid that it might have been Thaddeus come to say that John Emory had taken poorly again, she'd gone to the top of the landing to see who was there. Instead, it was Jessie Forbes standing in the doorway, and Martin Beecher was blocking her way. Hannah thought from Jessie's expression that she might shoot him.

"Why has she come?" Martha repeated distractedly, hastily dressing.

"I expect she wants to see Kate."

"Impossible," Martha said firmly.

"I don't think she's going to go away, Martha," Hannah said softly.

"No, I suppose not," Martha said in a strange voice, amazed at the strength of the bond between her daughter and this unusual young woman. She slipped her hand into the pocket of the apron she wore and handed a folded paper to Hannah. "I found this on Kate's bedside table yesterday."

Hannah carefully unfolded the much-read note and studied the message written there. *Oh Lord,* she thought as she read. *Poor Kate.* When she finished, she slowly handed it back to Martha. She wasn't sure what to say, so she waited for Martha to speak.

"Kate was going to run away," Martha said, clearly shocked. by the idea. She looked at Hannah with a weary pain in her eyes. "Can you imagine? She was simply going to disappear somewhere with that...woman."

"Seems they care for one another," Hannah said carefully.

Martha looked at her in surprise. "But to leave us like that. Kate must have been ill, not thinking clearly." But she didn't sound convinced.

"Kate has a sound head on her, Martha. She left that note because she loves you and Martin. She didn't want you to worry too much."

"You're not saying that you approve, are you?" Martha asked in astonishment.

"It's not for me to approve or disapprove. I just think that

Kate knows her own mind." With a faint smile she added, "Can't imagine where she gets that stubborn streak from."

"So, you think that we should encourage this madness? That I should allow that young woman to see Kate?" Martha queried defensively. *Oh, if only we had never left Boston.*

"Martha," Hannah said quietly, "I lost my three youngest in the epidemic of '52. It's a sorrow you never get over, burying a child." She saw the expression of pain and fright in Martha's face and regretted causing it, but she continued on, fearing Kate's loss more than Martha's anger. "Love has strange power. I've even known it to heal. If Jessie Forbes can keep Kate with you, I'd surely say pride had no place in the matter."

Martha stared at her wordlessly. Kate had barely been conscious the last twelve hours, and when she had managed any words at all, she had whispered Jessie's name. *Hannah is right.* If there were any chance under heaven that this young woman could make a difference—well, she'd worry about the rest of it later. She turned determinedly toward the stairs. "Thank you, Hannah," she murmured as she hurried past.

⌘ ❖ ♦ ❖ ♦ ❖ ♦ ⌘

Jessie faced Martin in the doorway. She was very close to losing all control. "I must see Kate," she repeated, her voice dangerously low.

Martin continued to stand in her way, his grief overpowering all reason. He couldn't think of anything except that Kate had planned to run away and leave them, and now she might truly leave them. Forever. "Kate is going to die in peace!" he shouted, his anger at this monstrous injustice seeking any object upon which to vent his rage.

"No. Please." The distraught rancher passed a quivering hand over her eyes, unable to bear his words. "Just let me see her."

"Why," he asked harshly, "what can you do?"

Jessie met his gaze, her face filled with torment. "I love her. Please, I—"

"Get out," he ordered stonily.

She could bear the agony no longer. She would not let Kate go this way. She could not. "Get out of my way or I'll kill you." Reaching reflexively for her revolver, she did not draw it, some last fragment of sanity stilling her hand.

Martha gasped, uncertain from the look on Jessie's face whether she meant to shoot Martin or herself. She descended the last few steps and stepped angrily between them. "Stop this, both of you. Carrying on this way with Kate lying sick upstairs." She turned to her husband, her eyes resolute. "Let her go to Kate, Martin. What harm can it do now?"

Jessie was already past them, taking the stairs two at a time. She slowed when she saw Hannah standing in the open doorway. Stepping quietly past her into a dimly lit room, she found her breath suddenly short. Feeling nearly suffocated by the dank, heavy air and her own choking dread, she scarcely registered the valise standing open by the closet, nor anything about the room other than the slight figure in the bed. Her heart hammered so hard in her chest she thought this sound alone might awaken Kate.

There was an eerie stillness about the way Kate lay motion-less, eyes closed, face ashen and glistening with sweat. The bed-covers barely rose with each shallow, labored breath. Jessie knelt next to her, reaching out with trembling fingers to gently stroke the pallid cheek.

"Kate," she murmured, the word a faint cry. She closed her eyes for a moment, trying to steady herself, then spoke again, her voice stronger. "Kate, love. It's Jessie." She pressed her lips to Kate's hot palm, her own warm tears landing softly on the fragile skin. "Love, can you hear me?"

After what seemed a very long time and with tremendous effort, Kate's lids flickered open, and her gaze rested feverishly on Jessie's face. "Jessie?"

Jessie rejoiced. Kate was not gone. She would not let her go. "Yes, love. I'm here."

"I...tried...to come," Kate managed, wanting so much for Jessie to know that.

"I know," Jessie choked, drowning in her fear. She struggled for strength, gasping, "And when you are well again, we will be together always. I promise you, Kate. I promise," she repeated desperately. Her voice broke. "Please, Kate."

Kate's eyes were suddenly quite clear and very calm. She smiled at Jessie, and her voice held an odd note of peace. "I won't be going away with you, Jessie darling. You must be without me for a while."

"No, Kate!" Jessie shook her head, her body wracked with sobs. "You *will* be well again."

Kate shook her head weakly and raised her hand to Jessie's tear-streaked face. "Jessie, my only love. You must say goodbye."

Martha Beecher, watching from the hall, stifled a sob and turned away as Jessie leaned over to press her lips to Kate's. This moment was not hers to witness.

Chapter
28

As the darkest hours of night enshrouded the Beecher home, Martha returned to Kate's room. She entered silently, stopping at the sound of soft words murmured in quiet desperation. Jessie was still on her knees at Kate's bedside, her head bowed over Kate's still figure, both her hands clasping Kate's. She was no longer crying, but her voice cracked with anguish.

"Kate," she implored, sure that somewhere Kate heard her. "I love you. Oh Lord, Kate, I don't know how I'll..." She brushed at the tears that fell again, drawing a shaky breath. She couldn't let Kate die being worried for her. She straightened her shoulders, but with each word, it felt like a little bit of her was dying, too. "It will be all right, Kate. I will never leave you, I swear. I will wait here, or hereafter, however long it need be. I am here, love."

Martha placed her hand gently on Jessie's trembling shoulder, shocked at her frailty. Her hard strength seemed to have dissolved as Kate's life slipped away. "Jessie," she murmured, her anger and suspicion disappearing in the face of Jessie's torment. "Let it go, child. The Lord will do His bidding."

Jessie turned to the woman in mute despair. Martha was stunned by the desolation in her eyes, and, instinctively, she reached out to comfort a suffering soul. She wrapped Jessie in

her arms, holding her while she cried, rocking her and stroking
her damp face. At last, Martha led Jessie stumbling to a chair by
the window.

"Wait here. We will know by morning," Martha said hollowly. She took a chair by Kate's bedside to keep vigil. Absently,
she reached for the thin leather volume that she had found in
Kate's luggage. The book fell open to a well-read page. Martha
picked up the photo marking the place and studied the image by
the dim light of the oil lamp. She could see that Jessie had been
smiling at Kate when Kate took the photograph. There was a
carefree exuberance about her that made Martha's heart ache.
They were both so young, and for a moment she forgot that they
were two young women, seeing only the love she could not deny.
She read the poem that Kate had marked with Jessie's photograph.

> *So are you to my thoughts as food to life,*
> *Or as sweet-season'd showers are to the ground,*
> *And for the peace of you I hold such strife...*

Her vision blurred and she could not go on, feeling as if she
had tread upon some sacred place. She looked from Kate's fragile countenance to Jessie's haunted face and prayed for them
both.

⌘ ❖ ◆ ❖ ◆ ❖ ◆ ⌘

As the hours passed, Kate's fever consumed her, draining
the last reserves of strength from her weakened body. Her
breathing grew more and more labored, and finally Martha rose
to find her husband, fearing that it might already be too late for
him to say goodbye. Her eyes met Jessie's, and Martha had to
look away, shaken by the agony she saw there. She had not
thought it possible that anyone, man or woman, could love so
unreservedly as that.

When Martha and Martin Beecher entered the silent room
just before dawn, Jessie stood by the window looking out into
blackness, her back to them, her face veiled in shadows. She did

not turn, knowing what they would find. She had heard when the faint arduous struggles of Kate's uneven breathing had stopped, and in that instant, a darkness deeper than night had fallen over her world. It would remain there, she knew, forever.

Martha's muffled cry, and Martin's faint groan, pierced her heart, and she closed her eyes. She could not bear knowing Kate was gone, even if it might be to some better place. For that she fervently hoped, but it gave her no comfort as the first terrible anguish of loss ripped through her.

In a moment, she thought, *in a moment I will go and leave them with their daughter and their grief.* She kept one hand braced tightly on the windowsill, uncertain that her legs would carry her from the room. Her body trembled uncontrollably.

"Martin!" Martha cried.

"Oh Kate," Jessie whispered in desperation.

"Is she gone?" Martin groaned.

I love you, Kate, Jessie thought, forcing herself to turn, wanting to see her, not knowing how she would say goodbye.

Martha stood with her hand resting on Kate's cheek, boundless joy on her face. "Her face is cool! The fever has broken. She is only sleeping."

Jessie bowed her head and wept.

⌘ ❖ ♦ ❖ ♦ ❖ ♦ ⌘

Seated by the bed, Jessie had Kate's hand in hers when Martha returned from speaking with the doctor. She brushed her lips over the open palm, then laid Kate's hand gently down upon her breast. Kate slept on peacefully. Jessie rose to face Martha, fearful of the news.

"He said that it will probably be a long convalescence, but there's good reason to hope she will recover fully," Martha said quietly, standing just inside Kate's bedroom door. For some reason, she felt as if she were intruding on something intensely personal every time she looked at Jessie Forbes looking at her daughter. There was nothing unseemly about it; only something so intimate, it made her uncomfortable. She hadn't imagined even a man and a woman could share such feeling.

"I'll be going now," Jessie said softly. She could barely manage the words. She was worn beyond exhaustion. Empty.

Martha stared from Jessie's tortured eyes to Kate, deep in healing sleep. She said nothing. It was best—at least it would be in time—if this could end now.

"Will you tell her I was here?" Jessie asked, brushing sweat from her face with a trembling hand. "Please?"

"I think it would be best if I didn't."

The words struck like a blow, and Jessie's eyes flickered closed for a moment. She steadied herself with one hand on the edge of the bedside table. When she recovered her breath, she met Martha's gaze directly. "Would it? Is hurting her ever for the best?"

Martha looked away, remembering the words Kate had written in the farewell letter. *"I love her, more than I will ever love anyone else in my life. I need to be with her, or my life will not be worth living."* Surely, surely, Kate could not have meant that. "What would you give to make her happy?" Martha asked suddenly.

"Anything," Jessie answered immediately.

"Then go, leave her. Let Kate alone to live the life she should." The words were spoken pleadingly, with no anger. Martha had seen enough to know that there was no sin between them, only an ill-advised affection. Women were not meant to live for passion, or even happiness, but to do their duty. Kate would simply have to accept that.

"Mrs. Beecher," Jessie said steadily, mustering all the strength she had left. "If Kate tells me to go, I swear to you that I will never see her again."

"And if she does not?" Martha asked wearily.

"Then there is nothing and no one who will keep me from her. If you send her away, I will find her. I promised her that I would never stop loving her." She looked one last time at Kate and then slowly walked past Martha toward the stairs. "I meant it."

Chapter 29

A steady rapping on the door awakened Jessie. She looked around the room, trying to figure out where she was and how she got here. She was on a bed, still in her clothes, her hat and gunbelt on the chair nearby. Her head ached and her stomach was queasy. She turned toward the window. It looked like it was late in the day, and as she struggled to orient herself, the rapping came again.

"Come in," she croaked. She cleared her throat and tried again. "Come in." She swung her legs over the side of the bed but didn't feel steady enough to stand just yet. Mae came in carrying coffee and toast on a tray, and Jessie could have kissed her.

"Lord, that smells good." Jessie groaned.

Mae sat down on the bed next to Jessie and set the tray between them. "Well, you look a mite better than this morning but not by much. Drink some of that. You need it."

Jessie reached for the steaming cup, vaguely recalling that she had stumbled into the hotel just after dawn. Mae had still been up. She remembered Mae's arm around her waist, helping her up the stairs. And Mae laying her down, and starting to unbutton her shirt.

"Thanks," Jessie said at length. "For last night...this morning, I mean."

"How are you, Jess?" Mae asked. It didn't seem to her that the sleep had done Jessie much good. Her eyes were darkly shadowed, her face drawn and etched with pain. She didn't look quite as wild as when Mae had seen her out at the ranch, but she was still far from right. "How's Kate?"

A faint light of happiness flared in Jessie's eyes. "She's better, Mae. Doc says..." She faltered, her throat suddenly tight, and she looked away. In a minute she continued, "Doc says she will get well."

Mae put her hand gently on Jessie's arm. "That's fine, Jess," she said, meaning it. "That's fine."

"Yes." Jessie nodded and stood wearily. "I should get back to the ranch."

"You should lay back down and sleep for two days," Mae said roughly, standing quickly, moving to stop her from reaching for her gunbelt. "You're in no shape to ride. You look like a good wind could blow you away. You need rest, or you'll be sick abed, too, and no good to anyone, least of all Kate."

"Kate?" Jessie asked dumbly. She was having a very hard time making sense of anything anymore. Just a few days ago, she had been set to leave behind everything she had ever known so that she might have a life with Kate. Then for long agonizing hours, she had believed Kate was about to die, and that nightmare haunted her still. She had no idea what to do next.

"You don't think you're the first person she'll want to see when she wakes up?" Mae asked with exasperation. "You're going to need all your wits to handle that family, and she's going to need you to be strong."

"What if they won't let me see her?" Jessie asked, her voice low and tortured. Lord, she was tired, and her mind was so muddled.

Mae cursed her own stupidity. *Why am I always taking Kate's side in all of this? Why didn't I just ignore Jessie's protests and finish undressing her this morning? I should have just crawled into that bed next to her the way I've been wanting to do for years, and maybe then Jessie would have given up this damn fool idea of being with Kate Beecher.* She looked at Jessie and knew why she had done none of those things. Jessie loved Kate, and there was no changing it. She sighed.

"Montana, I don't believe there's a man alive who could stop you from doin' something if you set your mind to it. You said so yourself just a bit ago. Once you get some sleep, you'll know what to do."

She put her arm around Jessie's shoulders and directed her back to the bed. Jessie followed without objection, and even let Mae remove her shirt and pants. Smiling faintly when Mae leaned down and kissed her lightly, chastely, on the mouth, Jessie was already asleep again by the time Mae gently closed the door.

⌘ ❖ ♦ ❖ ♦ ❖ ♦ ⌘

Kate opened her eyes and lay quietly in the still room, listening to the sound of pages quietly turning. She was very weak, but there was no pain. In fact, she felt very calm, serene. After a moment, she moved her head on the pillow and looked at her mother, who sat reading nearby.

"Mother," Kate whispered.

"Oh!" Martha exclaimed, dropping her book in her haste to reach Kate's side. "Oh, Kate. We were so worried."

Kate smiled faintly. "I'm sorry."

"Hush," Martha chided gently, brushing Kate's hair back from her face. "I'll get your father. He's still asleep."

"Wait." Kate held tightly to her mother's hand.

Martha pulled the chair closer and sat, watching Kate worriedly.

"Where is Jessie?" Kate asked softly.

Martha hesitated, then answered truthfully. "I don't know."

Kate's expression darkened. "Is she all right? She isn't ill, is she?"

"Not that I know of. Don't upset yourself," Martha urged. "You need to worry about getting well. Nothing else."

Kate shook her head. "I need to see her. When she comes, be sure to wake me."

"When she comes?" Martha looked at her daughter in surprise.

Kate's smile was fleeting, but sure. "She'll come, as soon as she's able. I know that she was here. I can remember her voice. Her hands." She looked at her mother, knowing her expressions well. "You found the note, didn't you?"

Martha dropped her eyes. "Yes. We can talk about that later."

"There's nothing to talk about," Kate said faintly, suddenly very tired. "I will never change my mind. No matter what we must do, where we must go..."

"Oh Kate." Martha sighed as her daughter gave in to sleep. She despaired of ever changing Kate's mind. And if she couldn't, then what was she to do? She and Martin could not force her into marriage, and if she sent Kate East, what then? Would that be enough to keep them apart? Martha remembered the determination on Jessie Forbes' face and the certainty in Kate's eyes. She did not think so.

She had almost lost Kate to death, and the unthinkable agony of that near loss lingered in her mind. Kate had been returned to her, a gift. She would surely lose her, she realized, if she tried to stand in their way, and that thought was more unbearable than anything else. She remembered Hannah's words: *Love has strange power. If Jessie Forbes can keep Kate with you...* She leaned down and kissed Kate's cool forehead, whispering a prayer of thanks for her child's life.

⌘ ❖ ◆ ❖ ◆ ❖ ◆ ⌘

Jessie unconsciously straightened her shoulders as Martin Beecher opened the door. He stood looking at her for a long moment, as if making a decision. He looked years older. Jessie figured she didn't look a whole lot better herself. She had slept one entire day through, and when she had awakened, she found her shirt and pants cleaned and waiting by the bedside. She had dressed hastily and come straight to the Beecher's. Now, she waited for him to say whatever he needed to say. She was calm, resolute. Only Kate could send her away.

Martin stepped out onto the porch and closed the door. He searched his pockets for a cigar as he walked to the rail. It was starting to snow, and the air was very cold. He snipped off the end of the cigar and lit it as Jessie came to stand beside him.

"Strange country, this," he said at last. "So beautiful, but so deadly."

"Is it so different, back in Boston?" Jessie asked quietly.

Martin looked at her, surprised. "Not so beautiful. Maybe just as deadly, but it more often kills the spirit than the body."

She nodded, thinking there couldn't be anything much worse than dying inside while you were still walking around. The way she had felt when Kate was sick. "How is Kate?"

"She's very weak, and she'll need a long rest. The doctor said another episode like this one could be dangerous. But by spring, he said, she should be fine."

Jessie sighed, some of the tension leaving her body. Spring. Five months.

"Is it true, what she says?" Martin Beecher asked, his voice low, his eyes still fixed on the far-away mountain peaks. "That you love her?"

"Yes," Jessie answered firmly, without a second's hesitation.

"She says that the two of you will go away, west somewhere, if we try to prevent her from living with you at the ranch." He said it as if the words were foreign to him, bewilderment in his tone and expression.

"Yes."

Finally, he met her gaze directly. "Will you promise me something?" She waited. "Will you promise to care for her always?"

We will care for each other, she thought, but she understood what he was asking. "Yes."

"And you will not take her away from us."

Jessie shook her head. "No, I would never want to do that. Kate loves you."

Martin sighed tiredly. "Then I'll not keep you from her. I will not lose her to pride."

Jessie felt suddenly dizzy as a great weight was lifted from her heart. She drew a deep breath and then another, finally feeling the strength return to her limbs. "I'd like to see her now."

"She's waiting," he said softly. He did not turn as Jessie walked into the house.

⌘ ❖ ◆ ❖ ◆ ❖ ◆ ⌘

Kate was sitting up in bed, her eyes alight with joy, as Jessie came toward her. She frowned just a little when she saw the dark circles under Jessie's normally clear eyes. Then Jessie leaned down to kiss her, and she forgot everything except Jessie's soft lips and gentle fingers stroking her cheek.

After a long moment, Jessie stepped back and smiled. "Kate."

"Hello, my darling," Kate answered, reaching for Jessie's hand and tugging her down onto the bed next to her. She rested her head on Jessie's shoulder, wrapping her arm around her waist, sighing contentedly.

Jessie pressed her lips to Kate's temple. "Your mother is likely to come up here," Jessie warned. "She saw me on my way inside." She had been surprised at Martha's calm greeting. There had been something close to acceptance in her eyes.

Kate shook her head, holding Jessie tighter. "No, not this time. In the future, we may very well have a chaperone while I am living here but not this time. She knows how much I need you here now."

"Lord, I love you," Jessie whispered, gently stroking her. "When you're well, you'll come to the ranch?"

"Yes," Kate answered, drawing strength from Jessie's presence. "Soon."

Jessie hesitated, remembering Martin's warning about his daughter's still fragile health. Winters at the ranch were the hardest season of the year. She often couldn't get in to town for weeks because of high snows and frigid temperatures. She couldn't risk Kate falling sick again that far from medical care. "You need time to recover, Kate. And winter has come. You should stay here until spring."

Raising herself enough to look into Jessie's face, Kate wondered how Jessie could so easily accept that separation. "Do you imagine that I could stand to be away from you for five months?"

Her hand slid slowly over Jessie's chest, lingering over the soft swell of her breast, teasing her until she felt the hardened nipple through the cotton shirt.

Jessie's eyes widened and grew dark. "Kate," she whispered, catching Kate's hand in hers to still her movement. She tried desperately to ignore the pounding that had started in her belly from just that brief caress, aware that she had no strength at all to stop what Kate had begun. "I want you so much from just being here next to you. You'll kill me if you do that."

"Then don't make me wait all winter," Kate threatened, but she settled back into the crook of Jessie's arm, too tired yet to do more.

Drawing a ragged breath, Jessie thanked the Lord that Kate didn't know how near she was to losing all hold of herself. "I'll be gone almost two months before the roundup, up in the mountains with the men," she managed to say. "Won't get down to the ranch but for a few days here or there."

Kate knew that what Jessie said made sense. She could barely stand and would be no help at all on the ranch. *But so long!* She couldn't imagine being without Jessie's sweet touch all that time. "We'll have little chance to be alone," Kate warned, "if I stay here."

"I know." Jessie nodded unhappily. "And don't think I won't be suffering, too. But I'll ride into town as often as I can." She raised Kate's chin with her fingers, looking deeply into her eyes. "I need you, Kate. I need you to love me, the way we do when we're alone. Lord, how I need that. But I need you well and with me more than anything else." She swallowed, wanting Kate's reassuring touch to banish her fears and the memory of nearly losing her. But she knew that it was not time and closed her eyes against the fierce wanting.

Kate read the need in her face and heard the yearning in her voice. "Jessie," she whispered, aching to ease those longings. "I love you."

Jessie smiled and blew out a shaky breath. "Well, I guess I can wait a while for the rest."

Snuggling closer, Kate was suddenly exhausted. She might have to wait five months to live with her, but she had no intention of waiting that long to love her again. She closed her eyes and fell asleep to dream of their love.

Chapter
30

The people of New Hope slowly resumed their lives in the aftermath of the illness, but for many, the struggles had brought changes and a renewed sense of appreciation for each day's gifts. Martin Beecher, for one, spent lunchtimes at home, basking in the sound of Kate's soft laughter as she recovered. Never had life seemed so precious.

Kate grew stronger day by day, as content as she could be waiting for the times when Jessie managed to come in from the ranch to spend an afternoon with her. Never alone through the long months of winter, they shared devotions with a glance and made promises on a smile, the brief touch of fingers and the fleeting brush of lips their only caress.

As hard as it was to be near Jessie and not be able to touch her as she so desperately wanted, Kate found it was harder still to be separated from her. Each time they parted at the door, Jessie would lean near and whisper, "I love you, Kate," and those words sustained her, nourished her, and gave her hope.

Finally, roundup week arrived again, and Jessie brought her herds in to town for sale. As soon as Jessie's business was finished, Kate planned to return with her to the Rising Star. The week was as hectic as it had been the year before, and most of the time Kate had to content herself with watching Jessie from a distance. The anticipation of seeing her, and knowing that soon she would be with her, always, was sweet in a way she hadn't expected.

Now that it was only a matter of days, she could look at her and dream of her touch with delight. When Jessie caught her eye in the crowd or tipped her hat across the corral, a soft smile lighting her face, Kate's heart tripped over itself. *Soon*, she whispered, *soon*.

At last, the waiting was nearly over. The next day was the final day of the auction. Martin had gone out with Thaddeus to put the finishing touches on the newspaper, and Kate sat with Martha on the porch, listening to the far away sounds of cattle and men, knowing Jessie was out there somewhere. She closed her eyes, missing her. *Soon*, she thought again.

Martha sighed softly, her eyes on Kate's pensive features, mistaking her wistful expression for sadness. "Are you sorry, Kate, that we came here?"

"Oh no. I love it here," Kate cried, her eyes suddenly alight with the truth of it. "I feel as if this is where I was always meant to be." She glanced at her mother and added slowly, "And if we hadn't come, I would not have found Jessie." She saw her mother stiffen slightly and waited calmly for the words she had been expecting for weeks.

"Are you quite sure about this, Kate?" Martha asked, knowing that there was very little time left to change her daughter's mind. She had seen the valises standing packed and ready in Kate's room. "Life will not be easy. Not at all what I had wished for you."

"Tell me, Mother, what is it you had wished for me?"

Martha sighed again, searching for dreams long past. "You are my only child. I wanted everything for you—security, a fine home—the things that would make you happy."

"And love?"

Her mother looked at her closely, then nodded. "Yes, Kate. Love, if it were possible."

Kate smiled tenderly, her deep eyes glowing with the vision of Jessie. "Will you believe me, then, when I tell you that I will have all of those things, and more, with Jessie? She is all I want.

All I ever dreamed of."

"You have made your choice, Kate," Martha said with quiet resignation. "I know that now. I do not pretend to understand it, but I cannot help but believe you. I have seen her look at you and you at her. I know what love looks like."

"I hope someday that you will be happy for me," Kate replied softly, reaching for her mother's hand. They sat together then and let peace come.

⌘ ❖ ◆ ❖ ◆ ❖ ◆ ⌘

Jessie answered the knock on her hotel room door, still toweling the water from her hair. Just an hour before, she had finally concluded her business, paid her men their wages, and returned to the hotel to get cleaned up. She pulled the door opened and stared in surprise.

"Kate!"

Kate smiled delightedly at Jessie's astonishment and stepped into the room, pulling the door closed behind her. She untied her bonnet and placed it on the small dresser. She leaned back against the bureau, content now just to look at Jessie. Barefoot, Jessie was wearing a clean white cotton shirt and her levis, and her deep blue eyes were already hazy with desire as they met Kate's. Kate thought she had never seen her look so beautiful.

"I have been waiting patiently all week for you," Kate said teasingly.

Jessie's heart was hammering, and she was incapable of forming any thoughts beyond wanting Kate. It was the first time in five months that they had been alone together. Kate looked radiant, a faint flush of happiness coloring her cheeks.

"Kate," Jessie repeated, whispering now. She moved forward, closing the distance between them, unable to take her eyes from Kate's, knowing that her need was plain on her face. She brought her hands to Kate's waist, sighing as Kate stepped into her arms. "Oh Lord, I've been wanting you so much for so long," she managed, her voice choking as passion flared within her.

When Kate lifted her face, Jessie's lips were there. She pulled Kate tighter, gasping at the first sweet pressure of Kate's breasts against hers. Tenderly at first, with soft caresses and gentle murmurs, they welcomed one another. They trembled together, barely breathing, amazed at finally being able to touch. But it had been too long and their wanting was too great to join gently. Jessie groaned, suddenly on fire, and her hands came quickly to the ties on Kate's dress. She could not bear to lift her lips from Kate's but pulled roughly at the barriers between them as her tongue moved over and into Kate's mouth.

Kate made small urgent cries in the back of her throat. Her fingers were on Jessie's pants, pulling the buttons free, pushing the material down her hips. She was desperate for the feel of her.

"Wait, Kate," Jessie gasped, finally pulling her head back, shivering with need. "Help me get your clothes off. I can't manage it."

Kate laughed and unlaced her bodice hurriedly. "You, too," she said, "those buttons are contrary."

They watched each other undress, their breath catching in anticipation as each piece of clothing fell to the floor. Jessie's fingers fumbled at the buttons on her shirt as she lowered her gaze to Kate's breasts, captivated by the faint blush of her skin and the tempting tautness of her nipples. She abandoned her attempts to unbutton her shirt and pulled it off over her head, then hurriedly pushed her levis off. Naked, she stepped forward, intent on feeling Kate's breasts in her hands.

Kate followed Jessie's gaze and laughed in eager expectation. Stepping around her toward the bed, she said playfully, "Oh no, not yet. If you put your hands on me, it will be over far too soon." Kate drew down the covers on the bed and slipped underneath. She delighted in the consternation on Jessie's face, reveling in the sweet power she held over her usually confident lover. "And I have waited far too long for this." She held out her hand, her face glowing, and said softly, "Come love me slowly, Jessie Forbes."

Jessie came to her, standing by the side of bed, and whispered shakily, "I want you so badly, it scares me."

"It doesn't frighten me," Kate responded thickly, feeling the urgency deep inside herself despite her intentions not to hurry. "You could never frighten me."

Carefully, Jessie leaned down, and pulled the sheet away from her lover's body with one hand. As her lips touched Kate's, her fingers brushed lightly down Kate's cheek, along her neck to her chest. She ran her palm over Kate's breast, swollen now with arousal, and finally caught the nipple between her fingers. Kate moaned with the swift stab of pleasure, almost a sob, and Jessie fought for control. Quickly, she stretched out on top of Kate, her thigh sliding insistently between Kate's legs, moaning as she felt Kate's wetness spread over her skin. She braced herself on her arms, looking down into Kate's face as she moved against her, her breath suspended as her blood rose high.

"Next time," Jessie gasped, feeling the pressure boiling up within her and the tension rippling down her legs, "next time will be slow. This time, I can't wait."

Kate stared up at her, exulting as she watched Jessie's face dissolve with need. Her hands clasped Jessie's hips and pulled her harder against her thigh, each thrust bringing both of them closer.

"Neither can I," she murmured, her vision dimming as her muscles vibrated on the verge of exploding. Back arched, desperately trying to contain the uncontainable, heat seared through her. Her will crumbled as a sharp gasp tore from her. "Oh!"

With a strangled groan, Jessie's head snapped back, Kate's cry pushing her beyond her last vestige of restraint. Her arms trembled, her hips jerked violently, and, finally, she could do nothing but surrender. "Kate, oh Kate," she gasped.

As Kate came, she wrapped her arms around Jessie and clung to her, holding her safe.

⌘ ❖ ♦ ❖ ♦ ❖ ♦ ⌘

"Kate," Jessie murmured drowsily.

"Hmm," Kate responded, softly stroking Jessie's neck and back.

"It's late," Jessie said with a sigh, rolling away until she lay on her back next to Kate, their fingers still loosely clasped. "You'll need to be getting back."

Kate sat up reluctantly, pushing her hair away from her face with both hands. "I know. My mother is expecting me to help her get food ready for the dance." She regarded Jessie tenderly, stroking her cheek softly. "You *will* be there, won't you?"

Jessie smiled. "That's where you're going to be, isn't it?"

⌘ ❖ ♦ ❖ ♦ ❖ ♦ ⌘

Kate smiled at the wrangler who stood patiently at the food table waiting for her to fill his plate with chicken and potatoes. She had been so busy with the endless stream of people that she had barely had a chance to search for Jessie. It seemed that everyone wanted to inquire after her health and tell her how glad they were to see her up and about. Even Ken Turner, squiring a pretty young woman on his arm, had greeted her politely, though he hadn't lingered long. He had quickly stopped attending her during her convalescence when she had resolutely, in no uncertain terms, declined his offer of marriage.

Thankfully, the musicians were now playing, and people were moving away to dance. She wiped her hands on a towel and made her way through the crowds out onto the back porch of the meetinghouse for some respite. She wasn't tired, but she was weary of making conversation. It didn't matter how well-meaning her friends and acquaintances were. There was only one person she wanted to see.

The spring nights were still cool, but she welcomed the crisp refreshing air. She gazed up at the dark night sky, punctuated by bright stars, and thought that at this time tomorrow, she would be standing on the porch of her new home. Smiling to herself, imagining the joy of lying in Jessie's arms at night, every night, she heard the jingle of spurs behind her. She did not turn, but savored the memory of the first time she had seen Jessie and heard the jingle of her spurs.

"What are you thinking?" Jessie asked softly as she stepped up behind Kate and rested her hands lightly on Kate's shoulders.

"Of going home with you," Kate said with a smile, settling back into Jessie's embrace.

Jessie brushed a kiss into Kate's hair. "Are you happy?"

Kate turned in the circle of Jessie's arms and smiled up at

her. She lifted her hands and clasped them loosely behind Jessie's neck. "There's no word for what I am," she whispered. "I am loved. I love. I have everything I ever wanted."

"So do I," Jessie said, kissing her gently. *Everything and more.*

There in the moonlight, with music whispering on the wind, they danced.

Also available from
Yellow Rose Books

Safe Harbor
By Radclyffe

A mysterious Deputy Sheriff, the town's reclusive doctor, and a troubled gay teenager learn about love, friendship and trust during one tumultuous summer in Provincetown. Reese Conlon, LtCol USMCR, is the new sheriff who has heads turning amidst speculation as to who will be the first to claim her heart. Victoria King, MD has tried love once, and found the price too high to pay again. Brianna Parker, the teenaged daughter of Reese's boss, wants only the chance to live, and love, in freedom. These three lives become inextricably bound as each woman must risk their hearts, and their souls, for each other.

Other books also available
By Radclyffe

Love's Melody Lost

Victim of a terrible accident, famed composer and pia-
nist Graham Yardley loses her sight, her heart and her soul.
Wealth and fame mean nothing after the devastating loss of
her beloved music; her life is reduced to silence, darkness
and bitter regret. In a bleak mansion atop windswept cliffs,
the blind woman withdraws from the world, her once con-
suming passions now a source of anguish and fear. Then
Anna, a lost woman seeking a place in the world, comes into
her life and awakens feelings she thought were dead forever.
A fragile melody of love is played between these damaged
souls, a song made sweeter and stronger by the day...but will
their blossoming romance be destroyed by an outsider's
greed or will it succumb to the discord of Graham's tormented heart? Can she find happiness with Anna, caught up
in the fiery overtures and darkly gothic strains of...Love's
Melody Lost?

ISBN 0-9702127-1-2

Above All, Honor

Single-minded Secret Service Agent Cameron Roberts has one mission—to guard the daughter of the President of the United States at all cost. Her duty is her life, and the only thing that keeps her from self-destructing under the unbearable weight of her own deep personal tragedy. She hasn't counted on the fact that Blair Powell, the beautiful, willful First Daughter, will do anything in her power to escape the watchful eyes of her protectors, including seducing the agent in charge. Both women struggle with long-hidden secrets and dark passions as they are forced to confront their growing attraction amidst the escalating danger drawing ever closer to Blair.

From the dark shadows of rough trade bars in Greenwich Village to the elite galleries of Soho, Cameron must balance duty with desire and, ultimately, she must chose between love and honor.

ISBN 0970887426

Coming this Winter from
Yellow Rose Books

Honor Bound
By Radclyffe

Secret Service Agent Cameron Roberts made a promise to Blair Powell, the President's daughter—not to place her own life in danger protecting Blair—but a request from the Commander in Chief forces her to break her word. In this sequel to *Above All, Honor*, Cameron places duty before love and accepts reassignment as the chief of Blair's security detail, despite knowing that this decision may destroy their tenuous new relationship. As the rift between them widens, more than one woman is happy to offer Blair the company that Cam cannot. Amidst political intrigue, an escalating threat to Blair's safety, and the seemingly irreconcilable personal differences that force them ever further apart, these two unusual women struggle to find their way back to one another.

Other titles to look for in the
coming months from
Yellow Rose Books

Prairie Fire
By LJ Maas

Many Roads To Travel
By Karen King and Nann Dunne

Strength of the Heart
By Carrie Carr

Red Sky At Morning
By Melissa Good

Northern Peace and Perils
By Francine Quesnel

Faith
By Anj

Thicker Than Water
By Melissa Good

Radclyffe is the cyberpersona and pen name of a devoted fan of lesbian fiction who lives and writes in the Northeastern United States. Since she read Ann Bannon's "Beebo Brinker" at the age of twelve, she has collected and written stories about the power and beauty of love between women. Although her works include mysteries, medical dramas, and political intrigue, common to all is the Radclyffe signature— high romance with a modern flare. A surgeon by day, her nights are spent writing and enjoying a true life love story with her partner, Lee.

Innocent Hearts is her fourth published work.

Printed in the United States
6902